W9-BJC-397

THE NOCTURNE MURDER

ALSO BY AUDREY PETERSON

**Victorian Masters of Mystery:
From Wilkie Collins to Conan Doyle**

A R B O R   H O U S E   N E W   Y O R K

AUDREY PETERSON

THE NOCTURNE MURDER

Designed by Richard Oriolo

Typeset by Fisher Composition, Inc.

Manufactured in the United States of America

10 9 8 7 6 5 4 3 2 1

Library of Congress Cataloging in Publication Data

Peterson, Audrey.
The nocturne murder.

I. Title.
PS3566.E765N6   1987   813'.54   86-17251
ISBN: 0-87795-862-9

AUDREY PETERSON

THE NOCTURNE MURDER

Designed by Richard Oriolo

Typeset by Fisher Composition, Inc.

Manufactured in the United States of America

10 9 8 7 6 5 4 3 2 1

Library of Congress Cataloging in Publication Data

Peterson, Audrey.
The nocturne murder.

I. Title.
PS3566.E765N6   1987   813'.54   86-17251
ISBN: 0-87795-862-9

FOR PAUL

1

I had been in London less than a year when I was arrested for the murder of my lover. At least, that is the way it would have appeared in American newspapers. In England you are described as "assisting the police with their enquiries."

It was on Friday, the fourteenth of March—a day I shall never forget—that I came back from the library to my room in Doughty Street and found the body of Maxwell Fordham lying on the floor. I could see that he had been struck on the head but I saw no sign of a weapon. When the police came I learned to my horror that circumstantial evidence made it appear that I had killed Max, and I was duly taken to the police station and charged with his murder.

But the story does not really begin on the fourteenth of March. The seeds of a murder are often sown long before the final act, and so it proved in this case. Perhaps I should have seen the signs in what I learned during the months before Max was murdered, but at the time I was simply bewildered. I knew only that I was innocent. I could not solve the riddle of what had really happened.

The year in London began with such tranquillity that the idea of my being involved in a murder was unthinkable. As a candidate for the doctoral degree in music history at my university in Los Angeles, I had been awarded a fellowship to research the subject of my dissertation: a study of Marius Hart, a little-known composer whom I planned to call the "English Chopin." Born in the same year as his great contemporary, Hart had lived on some ten years after the death of Chopin, composing music after the manner of his idol. My immediate task was to unearth whatever I could find of his music and to search for information about his life and work beyond the little that was currently available.

My dissertation director had helped me get permission to use the facilities of the British Library in London, including the music department, a fastness for scholars hidden away at the north end of the British Museum. Also conveniently close by was the excellent library of the University of London, where general and reference materials were available.

One day at the end of my first week in London, going down in the lift from the fourth-floor entrance of the university library, I found myself standing beside a red-haired girl in blue jeans with a book bag slung over her shoulders.

As I stepped outdoors I saw that the morning's rain had given way to the radiant sunshine of a June afternoon. The girl came out behind me, and we both stopped to savor the freshness of the air and turn our faces up to the sun. As we exchanged tentative smiles, I seized the opportunity to ask her about lodgings in the area. I had divided my week between work in the library and a fruitless search for a place to live and had learned to my dismay that there was very little available housing I could afford. Most students of the university evidently lived in the suburbs and commuted in by bus or tube, but I was still hoping to find something within walking distance.

The girl looked me over for a moment, apparently decided that I would do, and said in a deep, almost gruff voice that someone was leaving in the place where she roomed, if I would care to come and have a look. I said I would indeed, and we walked along toward the Tottenham Court Road.

"I have a bed-sitter over a shop in Charlotte Street," the girl said. "The woman who owns the place has the first-floor flat and lets out rooms on the floors above."

I asked my new acquaintance what her field of study was, and when we learned that we were both in music, our reactions were the familiar ones of intensified interest accompanied by a certain wariness. She was in performance—her instrument the cello—and as a performer she would suspect a music historian of being a scholarly bore, whereas I would be skeptical of a performer as a mere prima donna. We soon found, however, that such fears were groundless and an instant friendship sprang up between us.

Her name was Patricia Crawford, known to her friends as Patch. She had completed her degree at the Royal College of Music and was now concentrating intensively on cello study. When I briefly described my project to her, I saw for the first time the wry, crooked smile that was Patch's most endearing characteristic. With her red hair, freckled face, and tall awkward body, Patch would have been tabbed as plain at first glance, until that smile and the warm flash of her blue eyes transformed her countenance. On this occasion the smile was called forth by her reflection on my project on Marius Hart.

"You could publish that, you know," she announced. "Restoring minor figures to their place in the sun is one of our national pastimes."

I smiled back. "The thought has crossed my mind," I confessed, "but I have a long way to go."

As we approached the house in Charlotte Street where Patch lodged, she remarked with a kind of affectionate irony, "You know, Jane, my frightful landlady will be impressed with you."

I thought I knew what she meant. In my last two or three years of graduate study I had stopped wearing blue jeans for out-of-house wear and was now clad in a light wool skirt, silk blouse, cardigan sweater, and fashionable boots. I carried my books and papers in a handsome leather briefcase. At my present age of twenty-six I enjoyed my conventional garb, while for Patch, who proved to be three years younger than I, jeans seemed entirely fitting.

In Charlotte Street, Patch unlocked the street door next to a delicatessen and we started up the stairs. When we reached the "first" floor (in America, the second floor), Patch whispered, "This is the Gorgon's den. She lurks about as we come and go. Let's go up and drop our gear and then we'll come down and meet her."

Leading the way up another flight of stairs, Patch addressed herself to the double locks of her own door, opening at last to reveal what seemed at first glance to be a typical student room, with water-spotted desk, faded lounge chair, bed covered with an Indian print, and a gas ring in a corner. Striking an incongruous note in the shabby room was a magnificent cello, glowing like a jewel amid the untidy piles of books and scattered odds and ends.

"Place is a mess," muttered Patch automatically, not in the

least caring. "By the by, the rooms are all bed-sitters. I'm lucky the bath and W.C. are on this floor."

I took this to be her obliquely tactful way of making sure that as an American I would not expect a tiled bath and shower in my room.

"It's just what I want," I replied, wandering over to look at the piece of manuscript on her music stand. I could see at a brief glance that it was atonal—there would be no conventional harmonies or sustained melody in this music, just the harsh austerity introduced by Arnold Schoenberg and his school almost a century ago and only now beginning to lose its vogue. The music was scored for cello and piano.

"Yours?" I asked.

"No, a friend is doing some things for me," said Patch, with her wry smile and a slight flush beneath the freckles. "That's one of his."

Student music, I thought. Oh, dear, I hope she doesn't ask me to admire it. Yet I knew that if this was a special friend, as I suspected it might be, I already liked Patch well enough to submerge my principles for the sake of friendship.

When we descended one floor and sought out the Gorgon, it was as Patch predicted. I saw the gleam of reluctant approval in her steely eye. Her stout body was stiffly corseted, and from her heavy laced shoes to her perm-crimped hair, she was the very picture of stolid respectability. Told that I was looking for a room, her face took on a look of crafty calculation.

"Someone spoke for the third-floor front an hour ago," she said regretfully. "However, if the person does not return with the money quite soon, I shall be free to let to Miss Winfield."

We discussed the rent and she was reaching for the key to show me the room when the "person"—a cheery but unkempt young student—arrived with his money and settled the matter.

"I am so sorry, Miss Winfield," said the Gorgon, glancing distastefully at her new lodger, "but if you will leave your telephone number, I shall ring you if something else becomes available."

I gave her the number of my small hotel and Patch and I made our escape, retreating to Patch's room amid the Gorgon's declarations of my desirability as a future tenant.

_ "She's all right so long as the rent is paid," said Patch, grinning, "but she hates my cello. Since no one in the house complains, her only recourse is to look pained when she sees me."

"It's a beauty," I said, looking at the cello where it rested against a chair.

"A gift from a rather decent old uncle," she replied. I looked around at the dingy room and wondered if the uncle was also supporting her studies. In my own case, a small annuity left to me by my mother, added to my fellowship stipend, gave me a sufficient income to manage comfortably but far from luxuriously.

I was sorry to have missed renting the room, as the price was acceptable and I would have enjoyed Patch's companionship. We chatted amiably over our tea and made a date to meet for lunch in a few days, and when I went back to my hotel I felt pleased by my new friendship.

Long afterward, I reflected that if I had rented the room at Patch's place the whole train of subsequent events would have been different. I would still have met Max, but all the circumstances surrounding his murder would have been altered and I might never have been accused of the crime.

2

T hree days later I found my room. I had met Patch for a pub lunch and then set off for a sentimental journey to the Charles Dickens house in Doughty Street. On a trip abroad with my parents the year before my mother died, we had visited the Dickens house. In subsequent visits to London I had never returned, but I felt now that enough years had passed to make the memory more bittersweet than painful.

The house looked smaller than it had when I was eleven, as houses often do after a span of years. Dickens himself, I remembered, had also found it too small for his growing family and had moved to ever larger houses as his prosperity increased. I dawdled among the memorabilia, bought some note paper in the shop, and wandered out into another day of June sunshine. Back in Theobalds Road I stopped at a news agent's to look at the advertised rooms to let. While I had not thought of living this far east of Russell Square, the area was not much farther from the libraries than was Patch's place in the opposite direction.

Why not? I thought, and sorting out my change, I tried three numbers, two of which didn't answer. The third was answered by a Mrs. Hall, who gave me an address on Doughty Street and said I might see the room then if I wished.

Retracing my steps, I found the house farther down the street and on the opposite side from the novelist's house. The woman who answered the bell eyed me dubiously. At that distance from the student quarter, my conventional appearance did not assure automatic approval, as it had with the Gorgon. Mrs. Hall was more concerned about my youth.

"I prefer to let to older people," she said. If she expected me to retreat meekly, she was disappointed, for I ignored her remark and asked to see the room.

"It is on the ground floor," she said challengingly, daring me to say that I preferred an upper story.

"That would be fine," I replied, trying my friendliest smile. This cut no ice whatsoever. With lips compressed in disapproval, she announced, "You're from the States, aren't you."

My mother used to say that when she first traveled abroad everyone recognized American ladies by their shoes. Now that all shoes seem to be made in Italy or Spain, our feet have ceased to be unique. Speech, however, is still an infallible distinguishing sign. My brief utterances had signaled my origin as clearly as if I had the Stars and Stripes tattooed on my forehead. I always found this amusing but slightly disconcerting.

I acknowledged that I was indeed from the States, wondering if I had encountered a confirmed anti-American.

"I see. And how long do you expect to be in London?"

"For two years."

This produced a slight thaw. Evidently her concern was more financial than racial.

By this time Mrs. Hall had produced a key, and now she led the way along the central passage to a door on the right under the staircase. Suddenly she paused and looked at me accusingly.

"You won't have your own bath, you know. The W.C. and the bath are on the first floor."

Oh, dear, I thought, what a dreadful reputation we have. In anthropology books of future centuries, Americans will no doubt be justly described as a culture with a bathroom fixation.

"Yes, of course," I replied, thinking guiltily of my home in Los Angeles, where my father and I each had a bath and there was another for guests.

The moment I saw the room I knew it was what I wanted. It was far from luxurious. The furniture was a cut above Patch's place but still plain—a small sofa of faded but decent chintz, a table and pair of chairs of uncertain age—but the effect was pleasant. It was an L-shaped room with a window at the left looking out on a tiny garden; an alcove on the right contained the bed and a nicely arranged shelf over the sink, with a gas ring and an electric teakettle. But beyond all this, what struck my eye at once was the extraordinary fact that standing against the inner wall beyond the alcove was a piano. An upright of ancient vintage, it nevertheless appeared to be in working order, as I learned when I sounded a few keys and ran some segments of scales.

"Do you play, miss?"

"Yes, a little," I said, not bothering to add that I had stud-

ied piano since the age of six and had miraculously escaped
the trap of wanting a concert career. I added that I was doing
some writing about music for which I needed a piano.

The beady eyes narrowed. "We have a very quiet house
here. We could not have music after nine o'clock in the evening."

When I assured her that this was quite satisfactory and I
wanted quiet for my work, she looked unconvinced but
slightly mollified.

The rent was higher than I expected, but the presence of
the piano more than compensated for stretching my budget.
In the end Mrs. Hall accepted me as a tenant, I paid the first
week's rent, and she gave me three keys—one for the front
entrance to the house, one for the room door through which
we had entered, and the third for an outside entrance to my
room that I had scarcely noticed until then.

The house stood on a corner where a small street called
Wortle's Lane entered Doughty Street. Black iron railings ran
along the lane beside the house and there was a gate opposite
the entrance to my room, with a space of only a few feet
between the street and my door. Although at the time my
private entrance held no significance for me except as a convenient means of coming and going without using the central
passageway in the house, it was destined to play a significant
part in the events surrounding the murder of the man I had
yet to meet.

By the time I had checked out of my hotel and brought my
belongings to Doughty Street in a taxi, I was ready to initiate
my teakettle. On the way to the hotel I had picked up a bag
of basic items—tea, coffee, milk, sugar, pastries for celebration—and now I curled up in the corner of the sofa to enjoy
my small feast. I looked with pleasure at the room, welcom-
ing this first experience of living entirely alone. As an under-

graduate at Berkeley, I had lived in a dormitory for the first year and then in various apartments shared with other girls for the next three. When I was accepted for graduate study at the university in Los Angeles, it was more convenient to live at home with my father, a professor of history, and certainly cheaper for him. His salary at a nearby state university was comfortable but not grandiose.

For nearly two years I had enjoyed a tranquil existence while my graduate studies flourished. Our reliable cleaning lady kept the house in order. My father and I snacked, nibbled, or cooked on our own, sharing meals only if our schedules happened to coincide. His lady friend, Gretchen, came and went, always pleasant, their long-standing relationship a delight to all. Busy with her own career in anthropology, Gretchen clearly did not want to bother with marriage, and my father was happy to have her in his life on any terms. I was grateful to the fates for giving us Gretchen, for I realized how miserable I might have been if my father had cared for someone who regarded me with jealousy or resentment. Gretchen and I were good friends, all the more so because she never attempted to take the place of my mother.

Then into my peaceful life came Brian. Remembering brought me instant pain and a familiar tightening in the chest. Was this why love has become traditionally associated with the heart, this physical response even to recollections? My life seemed to me to be divided into Before Brian and After Brian. I had been casually dating a fellow graduate student in music history, drifting along more in friendship than romance, when I met Brian at a party. We began to see each other every day. I don't think we ever said formal things about love. It was just overwhelmingly there. We spent a lot of time together, either at my house or at his place. When his roommate moved out, I simply moved in. By that time I had a small salary from a teaching assistantship, enough to cover my share of our expenses.

My father and Gretchen smiled and said they were happy that I was happy. I didn't know then that although they found Brian charming and intelligent, they shared some doubts about his long-term reliability.

At first I was utterly oblivious to any flaws in my idol. For most of the more than two years that we lived together, I overlooked everything—his habitual lateness, his forgetting to bring the food when it was his turn to shop, his indescribable sloppiness. And indeed these things would have been tolerable if the more important values had been there. But when my faith in Brian began to crumble, my world fell apart.

Brian's father was an electrician and his mother a hairdresser in a small town near San Diego. When I finally met them—after much reluctance on Brian's part—I realized that he was deeply embarrassed by their lack of sophistication. They were good, kind people, enormously proud of their brilliant son. At the time I met Brian he was finishing his doctoral dissertation in early American history and was then on a two-year teaching appointment while he applied to other universities around the country for a permanent position. His mother confided to me how proud they were to have been able to pay for his fine education. Afterward, when I tried to say how much I liked his parents, Brian was enraged and accused me of being patronizing.

Gradually I learned that Brian simply could not believe in genuine feelings because he had very few of his own. He lived by a few surface rules of thumb that enabled him to survive in a world he regarded with cynicism. He was also extremely possessive of his own belongings, and I had become one of them. Brian was obsessed with jealousy of men with whom I had any contact. Professors, colleagues, students—all were regarded as suspect, even poor John, the inoffensive friend I had been dating when I met Brian.

His pet hate was Andrew Quentin, the professor who was directing my graduate studies. In vain I protested that Dr. Quentin was still devastated by the death of his young wife the year before and was not looking for romance.

"Listen, Janie," Brian would mutter, "a young good-looking guy like that isn't going to sit around weeping forever. Don't be so naive."

I realized even then that Brian was incapable of understanding the suffering most normal people experience, but I buried the thought and simply avoided mentioning Dr. Quentin's name.

Brian was certain that if he took a job on the East Coast, as he hoped to do, I would at once fall into the arms of another man. At the same time, his flirtations with other women caused me endless anguish that he refused to acknowledge.

All of this, however trying, is commonplace among lovers. What I found really unbearable in Brian was his dishonesty. I knew almost from the beginning that he often lied about small things, whether he needed to or not. When I tried to reason with him about it, he just laughed and called me a prude or a victim of bourgeois values. He borrowed money from friends with no intention of repaying them, although he was now on a full instructor's salary, earning more than those from whom he borrowed.

In May of our second year together, he accepted an appointment for the following September at an excellent small college in Connecticut. When he was preparing to leave in midsummer, I urged him to clear up several long-standing bills for a stereo and some expensive clothing and was horrified to hear him declare that once he had left California the stores would have a hard time collecting, so why bother? We quarreled so bitterly over this that at last he agreed to pay the bills, only to please me.

Then all my anger washed away in the anguish of parting. The terrible realization for me was that no matter how much I had lost respect for Brian as a person, I was still hopelessly in love with him. He had only to walk into a room and my heart filled with joy. I loved his slender body, his thick fair hair and mocking gray-green eyes. In my teens I had read Somerset Maugham's *Of Human Bondage*, finding it moving but wondering in my innocence why poor Philip Carey couldn't break away from awful Mildred. Now I knew.

During the first weeks after Brian left, his letters and phone calls were ardent. "God, how I miss you, Janie," he would say. No one else called me Janie, and my heart turned over at the sound of the name. Then things began to cool, and by November I knew something was wrong. When I talked about flying east to spend Christmas with him, I encountered a barrage of defenses. He might spend the holidays with friends in New Hampshire. Why not wait until spring break when he would be less busy? I guessed at once there was someone else but I avoided facing the fact. Perhaps it would pass; give it time. But by February, when he had stopped writing, I called and forced him to say farewell, repeating all the empty phrases about remaining friends.

For weeks my life was filled with pain. I was living at home again, preparing for the big doctoral exams. How like Brian, I thought bitterly, to defect at such a time. Logically, I should have been relieved to be free of him, but emotions, as I was learning, do not follow the path of reason. I got through the exams somehow and was beginning to revive after a month of relaxation when in midsummer Brian came back. . . .

No, no, *stop, stop*, said my mind. Sipping my tea in my new room in London, I had allowed thoughts of Brian to run through their familiar groove, but at the recollection of last summer I balked. All the unhappiness I had suffered before was just a prelude to what happened that summer. Although almost a year had passed and time was performing its healing magic, I still buried that memory as deeply as I could.

3

R esolutely I put thoughts of Brian out of my mind. I picked up my tea things, started a shopping list with items like dishwashing liquid and tea towels, and began to unpack my belongings. I was delighted with my room. When I had pushed the dining table against the wall to serve as a desk, put a row of books and music on top of the piano between bookends, hung my clothes behind the curtain in the alcove, and sorted out the music and papers in my briefcase, I felt cosily at home and ready to plunge into serious work on Marius Hart.

The piano proved to be in good condition except for tuning, which I would arrange for soon. I picked up some photocopies of Hart's music that I had brought from the library

and began playing through them. While the influence of
Chopin in the music was unmistakable, Hart had an origi-
nality that offered a promising line to pursue. Some passages
were banal, and of course he was less inventive than the great
composer, but other passages showed considerable merit.

So absorbed was I that an hour slipped away without my
noticing the time. At seven o'clock in the evening the sun
was still high in the sky, making it seem like midafternoon. I
was still unused to the long days of June. When I heard a
knock, I broke off with a start, hoping that the piano had not
disturbed anyone.

Opening my door, I found a blue-eyed, attractive young
man standing in the passage.

"Miss Winfield? I'm James Hall. My mother asked me to
give you this." He held out a receipt for the first week's rent.
"I hope you will be comfortable here," he added, with a
smile of such warmth I could not believe he was the son of
the formidable Mrs. Hall. Probably a foundling, like Oliver
Twist, I decided.

As I settled into life in Doughty Street, I never entirely
overcame my surprise that James was so totally unlike his
mother. Mrs. Hall did not improve upon acquaintance. No
heart of gold was concealed beneath that iron bosom, nor did
she unbend toward me except on the rarest occasions. She
seemed to regard me with disapproval chiefly because I was a
young woman and ipso facto not to be trusted. James admitted to me later that his mother had taken me on only because
the room had been vacant longer than she wished and because she felt that as an American I would be unlikely to
cause trouble under the rent control regulations.

The household included two other lodgers: Miss Leach, a
bookkeeper, and Mr. Emery, an elderly barrister's clerk. That
summer we often shared the tiny garden at the back of the
house, and it was here I first noted a pleasant English custom

I have come to think of as permissive solitude. Mr. Emery had a chair under the pear tree, where, after a courteous greeting, he retired with his book. Mrs. Hall and Miss Leach sat on either side of a rustic table, exchanging an occasional remark while Mrs. Hall pursued her knitting and Miss Leach read a book or flicked through a magazine. I found I could take the vacant chair beyond Mr. Emery and read or make notes with no obligation to converse.

Mrs. Hall was very proud of her little garden, as well she might be, for it was a charming refuge in the crowded city. Under a leafy tree the flower beds splashed their bright colors amid bits of greenery. Her roses were lovely, and my admiration of them called forth from her a rare gesture of generosity.

"Cut some for your room, if you like," she said one day.

At my obvious delight, her expression conveyed an amusing combination of grim satisfaction and a suggestion that I was somehow a frivolous creature for making a fuss over roses. I knew that Miss Leach occasionally took some cuttings up to her room, but Miss Leach was clearly on Mrs. Hall's approved list, being solemn and fiftyish.

Sometimes James came to join the group in the garden, and then the whole atmosphere changed. While no one would have described James as handsome, his clear blue eyes radiated an irresistible liveliness. He would throw himself down on the grass at his mother's feet, remarking cheerily on this or that, and presently we were all drawn into the conversation. Miss Leach beamed, Mr. Emery happily swam up from his usual absentminded preoccupation, and, encouraged by James's smile, I would join in with the others. Suddenly James would depart.

"I must be off," he would exclaim, kissing his mother and waving a cheerful farewell to the rest of us. He lived in the basement flat, coming and going frequently but rarely staying for long. Without James as catalyst, our conversations in the garden usually lapsed and we subsided into our separate silences or drifted away one by one into the house.

During that first summer I became aware that Mrs. Hall's love for her son was obsessive. However brusquely she spoke to him, however severely she avoided any outward display of fondness, the light of pride shone in her gimlet eye when she looked at him. His breezy and affectionate manner with her was a perfect foil to her frosty nature, and in their presence one felt instinctively her fierce possessiveness.

Thus it was that when James and I met by chance one day in Theobalds Road and shared a pub lunch, we tacitly refrained from mentioning the incident to his mother. It was not necessary for either of us to spell it out; we simply knew it would be less awkward if we avoided the subject.

Over lunch James told me a little about himself. His father had been a solicitor until his death during James's first year at university. The house in Doughty Street had been in the Hall family ever since it was built in 1799. After her husband's death, Mrs. Hall had unhesitatingly taken in lodgers in order to supplement her small income from insurance and enable James to continue his studies. He spoke of this with such unassuming gratitude that I was reminded by contrast of Brian's selfish arrogance toward his parents.

James had gone on to complete his law studies and was now, at the age of thirty, an associate in the firm of his father's former partners. Once he began to earn a decent living he had urged his mother to give up letting rooms, but she liked having the extra money. He rather suspected, he added with a smile, that she also enjoyed ruling over her small empire.

James invited me to visit his office one day, and accordingly I made my way on a warm afternoon in August through a gateway in Theobalds Road and into the precincts of Gray's

Inn, with its fine buildings and spacious green lawns, where many of London's lawyers have had their headquarters for centuries. Following James's directions I found the ground-floor entrance to the offices of Hall, Dexter & Smith in a building which, James had told me, had been rebuilt when the original was destroyed in the war. The firm still kept the name of James's father in its title. Looking at the names on the brass plate, I thought that someday another Hall would be added.

James greeted me with his cheerful smile. "Jane, how marvelous! Come in and have a cup of tea."

His office was small but charmingly furnished. There was a deep-hued Oriental carpet, two cozily elegant chairs on either side of the fireplace, a cabinet with gleaming decanters and glasses, and a desk with the burnished glow of fine old wood.

Over our tea James spoke a little about his law practice and asked with genuine interest about my project on Marius Hart. We chatted amiably for half an hour or so, and after that day we continued to meet occasionally in the same casual fashion, becoming good friends with no hint of romance. I suspected that there was a girl somewhere, but neither of us talked about our personal relationships, past or present.

During the next month my life jogged along in a pleasant round of work and recreation. I went often to the theater and to concerts, occasionally with Patch, more often alone. London's incredibly rich offerings of music, ballet, opera, and theater were a constant pleasure.

Then I met Max.

4

Max and I met for the first time at a concert at the Royal Festival Hall on a Sunday afternoon in September. I had taken the bus to the stop by the National Theatre on Waterloo Bridge, walking down the steps and back under the bridge to the concert hall through a typically British misty rain. Whereas in southern California the inhabitants are aggrieved if the weather is cloudy and are utterly prostrate if it rains, in London gray skies have a charm of their own, and one quickly learns that rain is a way of life. The view across the river from the South Bank was always enchanting, rain or shine, and I sauntered along feeling my usual sense of exhilaration at being in London.

The acquaintance with Max began in the most commonplace way imaginable. I had arrived a quarter of an hour early and was in my seat reading the program notes, not noticing the gentleman in the aisle seat on my left. As I rose to let new arrivals pass, I dropped my program. The gentleman and I both bent to pick it up, collided, apologized.

"Here you are," he said, having retrieved the program from under his feet.

"Thank you very much."

"You are from the States?"

"Yes." I smiled, amused at his instant detection of my origin from those four innocuous words.

I returned firmly to my program, avoiding any further talk, as I believed that, unlike Americans, the English dislike striking up casual conversations.

The concert began with a brief contemporary work, rather dull but inoffensive, followed by Beethoven's third symphony, the great Eroica, directed by a popular young conductor whom I had not yet heard.

It all began well enough, with the grand opening and the dramatic moment when the E flat major chord moves to that daring C sharp, which has been described as ushering in the whole of nineteenth-century romantic music. But presently I began to feel uncomfortable. In the slow second movement the dynamics were irritatingly exaggerated. Some passages became so pianissimo that the music was almost inaudible, whispering and tiptoeing along in a manner I was sure Beethoven would have detested. Then would follow a crescendo rising to earsplitting heights that seemed equally inappropriate to the musical text. The scherzo went along pleasantly enough, but again in the great finale there were exaggerations of sound. The effect, it seemed to me, was that of an actor who overplays his role in a bid for audience attention. In the case of Beethoven, the thrust of the music was sometimes lost in mannerism.

This mode of conducting seemed to me to be on the rise, perhaps because the dramatics appealed to the popular audience or perhaps because conductors, especially younger ones, felt the need to depart in some way from more traditional interpretations of the music. In any case, I found it disconcerting and gave the Beethoven only a few courtesy taps of applause.

During the intermission I took out the novel I was currently reading and settled in for a comfortable twenty minutes or so. I noticed the absence of my left-hand neighbor only because I could easily move my knees to allow the passers to go through to the aisle. Max told me afterward that he had wanted to talk to me at the interval but the appearance of my book drove him straight off to the bar. So much for my theories about the English.

The Rachmaninoff Second Piano Concerto, which came last, was a delight—suitably romantic and played with considerable charm by a young pianist, a winner of one of the great Russian competitions. The conductor derived a satisfactory richness from the rather thin orchestral score without resorting to bombast, and I applauded enthusiastically.

As we rose to leave, Max stood aside as I left my seat and walked beside me down the stairs.

"Did you enjoy the concert?" he asked, bending his head toward me.

"Yes, very much," I replied, having no intention of expressing my thoughts to a stranger. He still walked beside me.

"I noticed that you applauded less for the Beethoven than for the Rachmaninoff," he pursued. "Why was that?"

Surprised at his persistence, I turned and looked at him fully for the first time. We had reached the landing where the windows look out over the river, and we stood there while people swept past us and down the stairs. I saw a slender man in his forties with irregular features, olive skin, brown hair beginning to thin at the top, a mouth that seemed to be perpetually suppressing a smile, and very warm brown eyes, which were now looking into mine with quizzical humor. Before I could reply, he took my arm in a quaintly old-fashioned gesture and led us toward the windows, away from the crowd.

"You are thinking," he said, "how very un-English of this strange gentleman to inquire into my opinions. Is he trying to 'pick me up,' as you say in the States? No, perhaps you think, he is too old?"

I couldn't help laughing at the accuracy of his reading. Although I had not formulated these thoughts, he saw in my face their swift passage through my mind.

"No," he went on, "I am truly interested. What, I ask, does this young American lady think about the music?"

This interest, this intense curiosity about people and ideas, proved to be one of Max's greatest charms, and I immediately fell under its spell. I murmured in a few sentences my objection to the exaggerated effects in the Beethoven. As he listened, Max's face became serious, intent. He stood thinking for a moment and then said, "Yes. Yes. Mmmm. It *is* tiresome, isn't it? I expect I have tolerated this sort of thing out of sheer laziness—too much trouble to object."

I had no idea then that his words had any but a personal meaning. It was not until our next meeting that I learned that he was the music critic for *Apollo,* a London weekly arts magazine, and hence his "tolerance" consisted in not having expressed this particular complaint in print. At the time I simply felt pleased that this rather pleasant gentleman took an interest in my opinions.

Turning away from the window, I began to move toward the stairs, thinking we had conversed long enough. Besides, I was meeting Patch for tea and needed to catch my bus.

"Good-bye," I said, smiling and holding out my hand.

As Max turned to say good-bye, there was something so casually elegant about his movement that I half expected him to kiss my hand in the Continental manner, but he merely shook it gently and, assuming that I was a tourist, wished me a pleasant stay in London.

Some two weeks later Max and I met again, this time at the Barbican Centre, where I had gone to hear the chamber orchestra of St. Martin-in-the-Fields. As I sat in one of the deep chairs in the foyer, sipping a glass of wine before the concert, I heard an exclamation of surprise and looked up to see Max smiling down at me.

"How delightful to see you again. I expected that you would have returned to the States by now."

"No, I am living in London."

"With family? Friends?"

"No, on my own."

"Are you waiting for someone now?"

"No."

"Look here. My name is Maxwell Fordham. My daughter was to come with me this evening, but a young man rang up and she went off. At nineteen she does not give Father first priority." He smiled wryly. "Won't you come and sit with me?"

"All right, if you like. But my ticket?" I held it up.

"May I take it?" He went off to the ticket window, spoke with someone who seemed to know him, and came back to take me in to our seats.

From the time of our meeting at the Barbican, Max simply made himself a part of my life. On that evening he drove me home, for which I was most grateful. I had planned to take a taxi—a rare indulgence—because the oddly isolated location of the Barbican Centre made it uninviting for either tube or bus at night. We stopped along the way for a drink, talking intently about the perfection of the baroque music we had heard. He invited me to a recital at Wigmore Hall in the following week—and so it went. Each time we met he would casually arrange another meeting, sometimes including a meal, sometimes for the theater as well as for music.

As we became friends, Max told me a good deal about his life. He was a victim of the famous-father syndrome. His father had been not merely a conductor but the now-legendary Sir Cyril Fordham, one of the great names in British music. Sir Cyril, who was fifty-six when Max was born, had died some years ago in his eighties, heaped with honors.

"It's odd to think my father was a decade older than I am now when I was born," mused Max one day. So Max is forty-six, I thought.

It had been a second marriage for Sir Cyril, whose first wife had died childless. Max's mother was a Parisienne, a charming woman whose death three years before Max still mourned. His parents had separated when Max was a child, and he had lived much of the time with his mother in Paris, except for his days at Harrow, which he hated, and Cambridge, which he adored.

I told Max of my fleeting impression at our first meeting that he was a Continental, and he was delighted.

"Oh, absolutely! I often think of myself as French despite my father's efforts to Anglicize me."

"Then you saw a good deal of your father?"

"Oh, yes, my parents were always on good terms. They simply went their separate ways." He paused. "As my wife and I do now." Again a pause. "Except that we remain together for the children."

I said nothing but I suspected that, if this was so, his devotion was more to his daughter than to his son. Although he often adopted the pose of the despairing father, the nineteen-year-old Sheila was obviously the court favorite. When he spoke of his son, Alan, his face took on a kind of forbidding disapproval that must have been chilling to a young man of twenty-one. Later on, I learn the reason for his animosity toward Alan, and then it caused the only disagreement that ever occurred between us.

Max had grown up studying music as a matter of course. From piano to violin to clarinet to oboe, he had quickly developed facility in each but was far too lazy to excel in performance.

"No one quite said that I was being groomed to conduct, but of course the figure of my father hovered like some towering giant over the scene. It was a dreadful bore at the time."

When Max made comments like this, I thought at first that his flippancy concealed some sense of inadequacy. Did he feel the agony of failure at not having matched his father's achievements? Later on, however, it seemed to me that this was not the case. He was perfectly content with his life as a dilettante. What he felt was more in the nature of irritation.

"People always wanted to know about Father. What was the great Sir Cyril really like in private life—that sort of thing."

This was exactly what I wondered too, but I merely asked, "Was he kind to you?"

"He was certainly not *un*kind. I think he often regarded me with astonishment as a phenomenon of his old age, a sort of additional responsibility in a life that was already filled to capacity. During the times I spent with him, he often took me wherever he went. I hung about backstage a good deal with members of the orchestra or wandered into the auditorium during rehearsals. Sometimes he took me abroad with him, when he was guesting or doing opera."

Max paused.

"Actually, Father became rather a problem in his later years. He had always had many women in his life, but he developed a kind of obsession with being admired. He could not tolerate rejection, nor could he bear anyone who dared cross him. In public he was always in control, but in his personal life he had spells of irrational anger that were impossible to deal with."

I gathered that as a child Max had been rather petted by his father's friends as well as by his mother's circle. Even now, if he became irritated by something, I would see a glimpse of the petulant child beneath the sophisticated veneer of his charm, but on the whole he was a genial companion.

Max knew everyone in London's music world. He often took me backstage to meet the performers and conductors after a concert. On one occasion he introduced me to the young conductor we had heard at our first meeting at the Royal Festival Hall. I was surprised at the young man's gentle manner and the seriousness of his conversation with Max about a work he was preparing for an upcoming concert.

"I was tempted to tell him you didn't like his Beethoven," Max teased.

"Oddly enough," I said, "I expected him to be rather arrogant and I was quite wrong. I liked him!"

Max never explained my presence to anyone on these occasions. I had rather naively supposed that he would introduce me as a music student or perhaps as a visiting American, but he merely presented me as "Miss Winfield" without further identification. After seeing him regularly for some time, I began to wonder myself how to define our relationship. Was I a surrogate daughter, as he had suggested at our meeting at the Barbican? Was I one of several pleasant companions with whom he spent time now and then? He made none of the usual moves toward involvement that might be expected from so attractive a man, nor did I invite any. After Brian, my emotions felt frozen in some Arctic wasteland, never to be revived.

5

P art of my project on Marius Hart included a study of the whole milieu of the first half of the nineteenth century—literature, history, art, whatever there was in the culture of the period that might have influenced a composer. Accordingly I had been spending some time at the Tate Gallery on the Millbank, studying especially the magnificent collection of Turners, with their transition from quiet landscapes to the wild torrents of color in the late paintings, and noting similarities in the development of the romantic impulse in both music and art at this period.

One day in November, after a morning at the Tate, I decided to have lunch in the restaurant on the lower level of the gallery. When I had placed my order and sat reading and sipping a glass of wine, I heard a voice saying, "Hello, Mummy, sorry we're late," and saw a young couple joining a woman at the next table.

"How do you do, Mrs. Fordham," said the young man. "I'm Frederick Morgan."

"How formal, darling," said the girl. "Do call him Fritz, Mummy. Everyone does."

I recognized the girl at once as Max's daughter from photographs he had shown me, but whereas in the pictures she appeared to be an exceedingly pretty girl, I was unprepared for the dazzling reality. Sheila was no taller than my own five foot five inches, with brown eyes and hair like mine, but there the resemblance ended. While I might have been described at best as "attractive," Sheila was quite simply breathtakingly beautiful, with enormous dark eyes, massed clouds of hair, perfectly cut features, and the delicately glowing skin that photographs can never reproduce.

I looked with some interest at Max's wife, Cynthia, and saw a slim and stunning woman, her fair hair artfully streaked with silver and worn with striking simplicity to sweep off the face and hang bell-like to almost shoulder length. Even-featured, blue-eyed, Cynthia was in her own way as attractive as her daughter.

The waitress brought Cynthia's plate.

"I've already ordered," she said languidly. "I have an appointment rather soon."

I was aware of the absurdity of my situation. There was no way to avoid hearing the conversation at the adjoining table, nor could I change to another, as they were by now all taken. Then my first course arrived and I resigned myself with some amusement to my inadvertent eavesdropping.

"Fritz can tell you about the New York thing," Sheila was saying.

The young man leaned forward eagerly, his mop of wiry hair bristling and his dark eyes focused intently on Cynthia.

"Yes, I've just come back from New York. Sheila has told you, I'm sure, that I am in a rock band. We're the Mogs. You may not have heard of us yet, but you will."

Cynthia simply stared back at Fritz coolly, not bothering to answer.

"Well, the thing is, we did some recordings in New York with a fairly good company and I have some contacts there. Ever since the Beatles, the fans in the States are mad about our rock groups. One of the chaps I know has a friend who is a top agent for Hollywood films, and I want to take Sheila there for a screen test, as you know. I think she has terrific talent as an actress, and I have already set up a tentative date. What we want to know is, can we count on your support?"

Cynthia looked at Sheila. "Have you asked your father?"

"Well, that's the point. I sort of mentioned it casually and he went up in smoke. You know Daddy, he thinks I'm still an *infant*. It's so frustrating."

Cynthia looked at her watch. "I don't imagine I have much influence with your father."

"Yes, but Mummy, if you're not absolutely against it, it will make all the difference. You know how I love drama school, and this is a chance I don't want to miss!"

The young people went on talking eagerly about their plans, Fritz urging the advantages to Sheila's career that might accrue from the New York connection.

Presently Cynthia looked at her watch again and began gathering up her things.

"I must go," she said vaguely. Then, as if noting for the first time that some answer was required of her, she added, "I suppose you are a bit young to go alone. Why don't you stay with the Caswells? They have a flat in Manhattan. You could give them a ring."

"Oh, good idea, Mummy."

"Thanks, Mrs. Fordham!"

When Cynthia had gone, Fritz turned to Sheila. "Good work. Your mother is with us."

Sheila shrugged and looked down at the table. "She doesn't really care what I do. She's gone off to meet her lover. I think it's disgusting."

Fritz reached out and turned Sheila's face up to his. "Sheila, my pet, making love is not disgusting."

"It is, it is! I hate all that groping and pawing about."

"Why don't you come back to my flat with me now and let me prove it to you?"

"Oh, Fritz, don't be so *boring*."

"Listen, my little ice maiden, some day you are going to join the human race, and I want to be there when it happens."

"Well, it won't happen in New York. The Caswells are super-straight. I think even Daddy will let me go if they can put me up."

And so it proved, as Max himself told me shortly afterward. Recounting his daughter's plea to go to New York, he added, "I don't much care for Frightful Fritz, but Sheila will be all right with the Caswells. They are old friends and adore her as if she were their own."

He was more concerned, however, when three weeks later it appeared that the agent needed another set of tests. Max grumbled, "That chap Fritz is altogether too aggressive for my taste."

I wondered if Max would ever like any young man who paid attention to his adored Sheila. Nevertheless he gave her permission to make the second trip to New York.

One day soon afterward Max reverted to his plaint. "Frightful Fritz has taken to hanging about the house now. The thing that irritates me is that he has had a perfectly sound musical training, and he wastes it on something called the Mogs."

"Have you heard any of his recordings?"

"Yes."

"Well?"

"Dreadful! And to think that we had a reasonably intelligent conversation about Mozart one day. I can't see for the life of me what Sheila sees in him. He's—well, he's simply obnoxious."

I smiled to myself, and we went on to talk of other things.

6

One of the most gratifying aspects of my friendship with Max at this time was his genuine interest in my project on Marius Hart. The young composer had come from his native Dorset to London at an early age and made a name for himself as a piano virtuoso, following in the footsteps of the Irish composer John Field a generation earlier. It was Field who invented the title "Nocturne" for a short piece with lyric quality and a tone of brooding sadness, a form both Hart and Chopin used extensively. Marius Hart began composing music for piano at much the same time the young Chopin in Poland was beginning his career. Both were influenced by the music of Field, and Max was fascinated by the examples I was finding of the parallel development of the two younger men. I had given him photocopies of some of Hart's early work, along with selections from Field and some early Chopin, and he agreed that the similarities were striking.

It was marvelous for me to have someone to talk with about Hart. I had tried Patch but she was too absorbed in her cello studies to take much interest in the details of my research. Max not only shared my interest, he also proved to be of great practical help. In pursuing available clues to Hart's life, I had learned that Hart's great-granddaughter, a Mrs. Lewis, was living in Wales, and it was possible that she might have letters or papers that would be useful to my research. I had written to Mrs. Lewis some time before and received a reply from a grand-niece stating that Mrs. Lewis did have some letters written by her great-grandfather but that she was not in good health and regretted being unable to offer me any help at this time.

"She didn't positively refuse," I had said to Max one day. "Shall I go there and try bearding the lioness in person?"

After a moment's thought Max said, "Why not let me have a go at it?"

"Oh-ho! Like the fellow in Henry James's *The Aspern Papers*, you will make love to the niece in order to get the letters?"

Max grinned. "There may be a less onerous way than that. I rarely invoke the name of the Sainted Father, but it might do the trick in this case."

Accordingly Max wrote a charming letter to Mrs. Lewis, mendaciously hinting that his father, Sir Cyril Fordham, had been interested in the music of Marius Hart as a part of the British cultural heritage and asking if he might send a representative to see any Hart letters in her possession.

It was receiving the reply to his letter that brought Max to my door one afternoon shortly before Christmas. He had never before arrived unannounced. Often we had met at the appointed place and sometimes he had called for me, parking his car in the lane and coming in through the gate to my side door. On those occasions he had merely stepped inside the door, and on our return I had never invited him in. Thus in the three months or so of our acquaintance this was his first visit to my room. In my long cotton housecoat and an old sweater, I felt dowdy in the presence of so elegantly attired a guest, but the letter from Mrs. Lewis drove all other thoughts from my mind.

"Sorry to call without notice," said Max, "but I knew you would be happy to see this."

He held out the reply to his inquiry about the Hart letters. Mrs. Lewis wrote that she had indeed found a packet of letters from her great-grandfather to his wife. Her health was much improved and she would be happy to show the letters to Mr. Maxwell Fordham's representative at some time after the holidays, perhaps in the month of January. She had been a great admirer of Sir Cyril Fordham, having heard him conduct only once in the concert hall but owning many of his recordings, etc., etc.

I was overjoyed. "Thank goodness they are letters to his wife. Even his tailor's bill would be welcome, but these should give some glimpse at least into his personal life."

I offered Max a sherry and we toasted the success of the enterprise. Over a second sherry, I went to the piano to show him the material I was currently working on. We had already compared some early works of Hart, which showed him developing along lines similar to Chopin before he could have known any of Chopin's music. Now I was looking at a group of three nocturnes by Hart, which had been published in London by Clementi at a date when it was certain that Hart must have been familiar with at least some of Chopin's early work. Max listened attentively, agreeing that certain decorative passages and bits of theme material were specifically

Chopinesque. As I played another passage from the third nocturne for him, I suddenly felt his hand upon my neck and looked up at him questioningly.

He bent over and kissed me lightly. "Ah, Jane, you *are* a darling. I've wanted to do that for ages. Do you mind?"

My feeling at that moment was utter astonishment, not at Max but at myself. What had happened with Brian at the end of the preceding summer had caused me to withdraw snail-like from human contact. With Max I had felt secure because for all his charm he had, until that moment, been impersonal. What astonished me was that when he kissed me I felt an immediate rush of simple pleasure. Not intense passionate desire. Not a sense of being carried away and unable to resist. Just a feeling of delight.

Max easily read this in my face and, sitting beside me on the bench, he began to caress my hair, my face, my neck, murmuring words of affection, while my mind kept repeating, How nice this is, how happy I feel. When we made love, I savored the warm glow of returning life. Like a patient waking from the anesthetic after surgery, I felt myself thinking in a kind of weak surprise, So I didn't die after all. I'm still alive. Isn't it amazing!

A few days later I received a brief note from Max. With exquisite tact he avoided protestations of love and merely invited me to a theater matinee the following week. Only the final A *toi* and his initial M suggested intimacy.

What surprised me about my own feeling was the serenity with which I regarded the whole affair. I did not burn with fevered anticipation, counting the days and then the hours till our next meeting. Far from being distracted from my work, I found that my concentration was unaffected. When I met Max at the matinee I simply enjoyed the warm affection with which he greeted me. With enormous relief I discovered that I felt contentment but no anguish. If we made love that day it would be lovely; if not, another time would do as well.

As it happened, Max had another engagement that evening—a family holiday gathering of aunts and cousins at which he was expected to preside.

"The children used to love these events," he remarked, "but now they think it is all rather a bore. However, Cynthia insists on their coming." He paused. "At least Horrid Hugh won't be there."

Whenever Max referred to his wife and her lover, the bitterness of his tone made me wonder if his wife's unfaithfulness had been the initial cause of their rupture. They still kept up appearances and went about together occasionally, but I sensed that Max deeply resented her relationship with another man.

After the matinee Max drove me back to Doughty Street, parking briefly in the lane beside my gate. It was already dark and the softly persistent rain outside made the interior of the car seem like a warm cocoon. Max kissed me gently, murmuring, "Dear Jane, dear darling Jane." He set a date for us to meet after the holidays, and as I stepped out of the car he handed me a small package beautifully wrapped in green foil with a red ribbon and a sprig of holly. In turn, I gave him the little book I had wrapped for him.

Max's gift proved to be a gorgeous and amusing silk scarf bearing the name of a French designer. The pattern in the center of the scarf was a scattering of scarlet elephants, while the border consisted of broad bands of color—green, gold, navy, white, and scarlet. The whole effect was charming and I loved it. I had also learned its usefulness. At home in California I sometimes wore a scarf over my head on a windy day, but in London I had found that scarves were invaluable for the constant misty rains, and I knew that this one would be my favorite for special occasions.

I spent the evening packing. Patch had invited me to spend a few days over Christmas at her home in Surrey. Except for a casual remark that it was in the country, so bring some boots for walking, she had given me no clue about how to dress. With her excessive reticence Patch rarely spoke of her family except for an occasional fond reference to her mother or a mention of her stepfather's liking for dogs. I guessed that they might be simple country people and accordingly packed a modest wardrobe, reluctantly leaving behind the dazzling silk square from Max.

My father had offered to send me the air fare to come home for the holidays but I had decided to wait until summer, breaking the two years at the halfway point. Before going to bed I phoned him—it was still afternoon in California—and felt cheered as we exchanged Christmas greetings.

As I left Doughty Street the next morning I looked fondly at the unpretentious room where I now felt so much at home. In my euphoric mood it would never have occurred to me that three short months later that room would become a scene of horror.

7

The next day I took the brief train ride into Surrey and Patch met me at the station, the crooked smile lighting up her face.

"Do you mind walking?" she asked, seizing my bag and noting that I had followed her advice and worn walking boots. "It's only a mile and a bit."

"No, I'd love it!"

There was snow on the ground, a novelty that enchanted me.

"When I was a child," I told Patch, "I had to be taken up into the mountains to see the snow."

"I like it too," said Patch. "Sometimes in mild winters we get very little snow and it's rather disappointing."

As we tramped along we fell into our recurring friendly argument about contemporary music. I had discovered that while Patch was deeply shy in speaking of personal matters, she reveled in battles royal about music.

"Did you look at the Lenski score I gave you?" she began. This was like saying *en garde,* and I came to attention at once, ready for thrust and parry.

"Yes, I looked at it. Of course I can see the structure of what he is doing. But since when is music a visual art? I thought it had something to do with *hearing.*" Heavy irony.

"You listened to the tape?"

"Yes. Over and over. It's frightful."

"If you keep wanting it to sound familiar, like, well, Tschaikowsky"—deep scorn—"you will obviously be disappointed. You must take Lenski on his own terms and listen to what *he* says."

"The problem may be that what he says isn't worth hearing!"

Anton Lenski was a contemporary Polish composer who had achieved enough recognition to have had a number of short works performed by various orchestras in Europe and the United States. I regarded these performances as a form of tokenism. Under pressure from certain quarters, many music directors feel obliged to demonstrate their tolerance by dutifully including contemporary works on their programs from time to time, often without genuine enthusiasm for the product.

"At least," I added to Patch, "Lenski's things are mercifully short."

Patch greeted this cynicism with howls of derision, but after a time we abandoned our friendly antagonisms and gave ourselves up to the charm of the snow-clad wooded countryside through which we were passing.

Even with boots, my feet were thoroughly icy by the time we turned off the road to our left and passed between two enormous stone gateposts and through an open gate. At the right of the drive, which curved off gently downhill, was a perfectly square stone house with no pretensions to architectural charm but relieved from austerity by the deep woods in which it stood.

"Here we are," said Patch, unlocking the front door. Her parents were evidently not at home, for she led me straight up the stairs, where there appeared to be several bedrooms.

"Here's my room," she said, dropping her gear as she went, "and here's yours. Bath's at the end of the passage."

My room was plainly furnished except for an enormous mahogany wardrobe, slightly marred and too large for the room, but clearly at one time a fine piece. Had her parents once been more prosperous, as with so many British people who live in genteel poverty? Out of the window of my room I saw the roof and chimneys of a large country house, of which this must be the lodge or gatehouse. Perhaps her parents rent this, I thought.

Patch, sauntering in to watch me unpack, announced that Mimi (her name for her mother) wanted us to come for a cup of tea at four o'clock.

"Your parents don't live here?" I asked in surprise.

Patch flushed a deep crimson, looking as uncomfortable as I had ever seen her look.

"No, they live down the hill." She gestured toward the house I had seen through the trees.

Perhaps they were employed at the manor house, with Patch allowed to use the lodge. How painfully aware the English are of class distinctions, I thought. Americans are certainly not immune to family pride, but we have a cultural assumption that our origins do not always determine our status in life.

I slipped into a plain green wool dress and in a little while we set off down the winding road, presently coming in sight of an immense house with an imposing Georgian front and what looked like a much older wing at the side. Patch led the way along the drive and around to a side entrance, through a maze of passages, and up a flight of back stairs.

Presently we emerged into a charmingly furnished room where a lady sitting before the fire looked up with a cry of pleasure.

"Darling! How good to see you! And this must be Jane."

The flush appeared again beneath Patch's freckles as she muttered to me, "My mother, Lady Muriel."

Patch, you idiot, I thought, why didn't you tell me? In anyone else, I would have regarded this as the worst kind of reverse snobbery, but I somehow understood that for Patch, with her painful reticence, it would have been impossible to "explain" her family. I smiled inwardly at my conjectures about her humble origins.

At first glance, Patch and her mother seemed totally unlike. Small and slender, with soft brown hair, Lady Muriel radiated a natural beauty of face and figure. Only in the dazzling blue eyes did one see the resemblance to Patch, who must have derived her reddish hair and large physique from her father, who had died when she was sixteen. Patch clearly adored her mother, and Lady Muriel, while gazing at her daughter with the little smile of slightly detached amusement with which she seemed to regard the world, conveyed a warm affection for her.

"Patricia, dear, will you ask Betty for the tea, please?"

With a slight start I remembered that Patch did have a proper name.

Lady Muriel smiled. "I've never managed to say 'Patch,' although her friends have called her nothing else since her school days."

From across the room Patch, apparently summoning Betty through an intercom, grinned. "'Patricia' sounds all right when Mimi says it," she said. She went to sit on the arm of her mother's chair. "Where's Dods?"

"Oh, tramping about as usual. He'll be along." And indeed, a moment later, a stocky man in his fifties appeared, dressed to my astonishment in the garb of an American cowboy straight out of the movies, complete with Western plaid shirt, silver belt buckle, and tooled leather boots.

"Jane, dear, my husband, Lord Dodson." The little amused smile appeared again. "He is a devotee of your films about the Wild West."

"Damned comfortable way to dress, I can tell you," he replied serenely.

When the tea arrived, Lady Muriel poured and Patch handed round the cups and platefuls of buttered scones. I sank back in my chair, enjoying my first taste of family life since leaving home six months earlier. As they chatted about their recent activities, I felt comfortably included in the casual atmosphere.

When her stepfather launched into a discussion about the current status of their kennels, Patch released me with the remark that "Jane doesn't fancy dogs." Lord Dodson, no doubt regarding this as an eccentricity excusable only in a foreigner, gave me a benign smile and carried on. With their last swallow of tea, the two went off eagerly "to see the dogs."

Lady Muriel smiled at me. "Will you excuse me for a moment, Jane? I must make a telephone call."

Alone by the fire, I looked at a group of magazines on the table near my chair and found a recent copy of *Apollo*, the journal for which Max did music reviews. Although its high price had put a strain on my budget, I had subscribed to *Apollo* soon after Max and I became friends and had been delighted with the magazine. Its glossy pages often had gorgeous displays of art and architecture as well as excellent theater and book reviews and illuminating articles on offbeat or little-known topics in the arts. And of course it was always interesting to read Max's reviews.

What I had learned about Max was also illuminating, in a personal sense. While his reviewing showed flashes of brilliance, his usually graceful style sometimes lapsed into the pedestrian, as if he couldn't be bothered trying to be more scintillating. He was essentially both arrogant and lazy. The weekly format of the magazine permitted considerable latitude. He was not required to cover all the major musical events of the week. He could select those items each week that happened to interest him, and it was clear over the course of time that he took full advantage of his freedom. Twice in the three months since I had taken *Apollo* his column had failed to appear. I remembered that I had told him on the first occasion that I missed seeing his contribution, to which he had airily remarked that his editor didn't like it "but he tolerates me." He often complained of the irksomeness of the deadline, and after the second omission I said nothing.

Turning the pages of Lady Muriel's copy of *Apollo*, I paused at Max's column and was reading it when she returned. From her chair at my side she glanced over and remarked, "Ah, Maxwell Fordham! Have you read his things? He *can* be so clever when he bothers."

I looked up in surprise at the analysis so close to my own.

"Dear Max," she went on, her beautiful face alight with a smile that seemed to reflect wryly on life's oddities. "I've known him for simply ages. My brother was at Kings College with Max and sometimes brought him home. I was younger and a bit infatuated, I think. He was so charming. Then we each married and of course we often met by chance in music circles. In London one keeps seeing the same people everywhere, doesn't one?" She paused, gazing into the fire. "After Patricia's father died, Max was very kind . . . very kind."

I sat quite still, transfixed with indecision. It seemed impossible not to acknowledge my acquaintance with Max. Had it been even a short time earlier, before our relationship changed, I might have done so casually enough, but now I seemed unable to speak without feeling awkward. Lady Muriel had not said "Max and his wife" were kind, and her continued reverie, oblivious to my presence, made it easy enough to guess that it was Max alone whose consolation, whatever its form, had been offered.

Before I could formulate a reply, Lady Muriel changed the conversation and the subject of Max was abandoned.

The week I spent with Patch and her family made a memorable holiday for me. Sometimes I went with Patch for long walks through the snowy woods and fields. Sometimes we drove into the village with Dods and returned laden with items from a long shopping list. We played a lot of music, to which Lady Muriel listened with keen interest, making perceptive comments from time to time. I learned that she was a sponsor of a number of music groups in London and throughout the British Isles, not merely as a contributor of funds but as an active participant in all sorts of endeavors.

On Christmas Eve there was a gathering of family and friends at the great house. Everyone helped to trim the tree, and we gorged ourselves on food and wine from the enormous buffet table.

On my last evening we dined at the Hall and I took my

leave of Patch's parents. When at last we retreated to her gatehouse, Patch lit a fire in the ground-floor parlor and we curled up in robes and slippers to sip a nightcap. I remarked on the charm of her gatehouse, and she broke into her warm crooked smile.

"It was awfully decent of Dods to let me have it. No one can afford resident gardeners anymore, nor did he want to let it to strangers. So Mimi fixed it up for me two years ago for my twenty-first birthday."

Although Patch and I rarely exchanged confidences, I had told her briefly about Brian, and now she surprised me by divulging that in the previous year her cottage had been the meeting place for a brief but torrid love affair. At least, this was my interpretation of the rather halting and cryptic phrases with which she referred to the event.

Patch did not identify her lover, but I was certain that it was the Jeremy who had composed the atonal cello composition I had first seen on the music stand in her room in Charlotte Street. I had met Jeremy one day when Patch and I were in a bookstore in Great Russell Street. Her diffidence in Jeremy's presence, while not unusual for Patch, revealed a special kind of fondness. Certainly she admired his talent and regarded him as a coming genius of the music world. I had found Jeremy quite a charming member of what I thought of as the Young Bearded set, but our meeting was too brief for more than a fleeting impression.

When Patch asked if I missed being at home for the holidays, I realized that in answering her question I was able to assess my own sense of progress in recovering from the affair with Brian. Patch's rather touching confidence about her love affair had brought us closer than we had been before.

"Of course," I began, "I would like to be with my father and Gretchen, and to see old friends, but I think it's best to be away for as long as possible. Going back now might awaken feelings that are better left dormant."

I held out my glass for more brandy.

"It's odd how the sheer distance helps in some way. If I were in California now, I would be terrified that Brian might turn up."

"You wouldn't want to see him?"

"No, I would hate it. I simply don't know whether I would be able to refuse."

I wanted to tell Patch about Max, but it seemed too fragile a topic for discussion. At this point I was not at all sure what I thought about it myself. I had not told Patch earlier about my acquaintance with Max out of an odd sense that it might sound like name-dropping. Now, having learned that Lady Muriel had known Max, perhaps intimately, I felt it was doubly impossible. Instead, I turned to a question I had been wanting to ask ever since my arrival at the Hall.

"I know almost nothing about titles, Patch. Do you mind my asking? I would have thought that Mimi would be 'Lady Dodson'—or is she?"

Patch grinned. "It's all a lot of nonsense, really, but what can one do? You see, Grandfather—Mimi's father—was the Earl of Waite, and earls' daughters have a title in their own right. So Mimi is Lady Muriel. If the title were through marriage alone she would be Lady Dodson. As it is, she is Lady Muriel Dodson."

Now it was my turn to smile. "And what about earls' granddaughters?"

"Oh, I'm the Honorable Patricia, but I keep it rather dark."

We giggled. "Your secret is safe with me."

Patch went on to speak of her father. "He was an excellent pianist and we used to play together. My uncle—his

brother—played the violin. He gave me my first cello when I
was quite small so that we could have a family trio. Mimi
loved it when I was able to hold my own with them. She
plays no instrument, but she is very knowledgeable about
music, as you've seen."

"Your mother is so lovely," I said. "I'm glad she has found
someone as nice as Dods."

"Actually, everyone was a bit surprised when she married
him. Of course he was mad about her after Father died, but
she scarcely seemed to notice him for ages. I was away at
school at the time but I remember at holidays that he was
always standing by, sort of worshiping from a respectful distance. Then suddenly one day she accepted him and off they
went to his place in Scotland for the shooting. Can you believe it?"

I confessed that I found it hard to imagine the delicate
Lady Muriel stuffing bleeding pheasants into a bag. Lord
Dodson did seem to be a classic illustration of those aristo-
crats whom Matthew Arnold, that eminent Victorian, had
dubbed "Barbarians" because of their love of field sports.

"In fact," Patch went on, with her warm smile, "Dods has
been absolutely marvelous to me, and Mimi seems very
happy with her life."

Our talk turned, as it inevitably did, to music. We had
been playing through Chopin's sonata for cello and piano,
finding it delightfully rewarding and wondering why it was so
seldom performed. On any topic except contemporary music,
Patch and I had found that we shared all sorts of enthusi-
asms. Unlike many musicians who were chiefly performers,
she had wide and eclectic tastes and a broad comprehension
of music beyond the repertoire of her own instrument.

I told Patch about the letters of Marius Hart I hoped to see
in Wales. Now Patch said thoughtfully, gazing into the fire,

"You see, Jane, for more than a century Marius Hart's music has faded out and remained unrecognized, and now he, and other composers like him, may come in for a revival. In the same way, composers like Anton Lenski may be unappreciated today but a century from now they may come into their own."

In the mellow mood induced by the brandy and even more by my fondness for Patch, I refrained from uttering a sharp retort, which would have been my usual response. Instead, I murmured vaguely that one never knew.

8

Back in London, I met Max's son, Alan, for the first time. I had found a note from Max confirming our luncheon date for the following day, and when Max called for me at the north entrance to the British Museum, he explained that he had to drop off the copy for this week's column at the *Apollo* office before going on to lunch. His zippered case lay beside him on the seat of the car as we moved along through the London traffic, but suddenly he exclaimed, "Oh, damn! I left the stuff at home on my desk. Do you mind if we go back for it?"

"Of course not."

"Probably no one is there at the moment. Sheila is at her drama school. Alan is rarely at home. And Cynthia has gone to the Riviera for two weeks. No doubt Horrid Hugh will be there with her."

"Is he really so horrid?" I asked with a smile.

Max grinned with the impish expression of a child caught in a fib. "No, actually he's a decent enough chap, but I'm sure I don't know what she sees in him."

A frown creased his brow, and his face took on the petulant look that always appeared at the thought of his wife's lover.

We drove north past Regent's Park and into Hampstead. In one of the streets leading up the hill toward the High Street, Max turned into the drive of a graceful and elegant house.

"It's lovely," I exclaimed.

"I've always been fond of it. It hasn't been in the family for long. Actually, the Sainted Father bought it when he and Maman were married, and thank heaven he kept it on after she went to live in Paris." Pause. "I suppose now it will have to go to Alan."

I wondered at the bitterness of his tone. And at that moment a fair-haired and handsome young man emerged from a basement door and opened the garage in front of Max's car. Max stepped out, walked around to my side of the car, and gestured for his son to come to us. As Alan acknowledged the introduction, I formed an instant impression of a likable young man.

"I'm going straight out," said Max to his son. "I must pick up some papers in the house."

"Yes, of course. No rush."

"I won't be a moment."

Despite the trivial nature of the remarks exchanged, there was a strong sense of antagonism between the two. Both spoke with an excessive and measured courtesy that only emphasized the coldness of their voices. It seemed to me this

was more than the usual tension of generation-gap differences.

As Max walked toward the house, Alan bent down to speak
to me.

"Are you from the States, Jane?" he asked, all the coolness
gone from his face with his father's departure.

We exchanged a few friendly remarks, smiling at each
other with a sense of spontaneous accord. He had come
down from Cambridge that summer and was "dabbling," as
he put it, in stage design.

"My sister, Sheila, is at drama school and I have done one
or two things there."

We smiled good-bye as Max returned.

"Max, he's a darling!" I said, as we drove down the hill.

Max simply snorted and changed the subject, leaving me
puzzled but unwilling to pursue the matter.

"Did you enjoy your holiday in the country?" he asked.

"Yes, very much." I hesitated. If Max had asked me with
whom I had visited, I would have told him about meeting
Lady Muriel, but he expressed no interest in what he obviously took to be a dull time with a young friend, so I said
nothing more.

Over lunch we talked about my visit to Wales, which had
been tentatively arranged for January. Suddenly he reached
out and took my hand across the table, his face glowing.

"Jane, shall I come too? Let me arrange it as a holiday for
us. Would you like that?"

I was pleased by his tact. He was asking my consent, not
merely taking it for granted, as a younger man might do, that
our one occasion of intimacy guaranteed its continuance.

Accordingly, a week later Max and I set off, having confirmed the appointment with Mrs. Lewis, to see the Marius
Hart letters. When Max called for me at about half past eight
in the morning, he parked in the lane and came in for a cup

of coffee while I gathered my things together. I tied on the silk scarf he had given to me at Christmas, the scarlet elephants marching cheerily over the top of my head. Minutes later we emerged from the gate, and as Max lifted my overnight bag into the boot of his car, Miss Leach walked briskly past, evidently on her way to her office. Her eyes took in the scene, and with compressed lips and something close to a sniff she muttered "Good morning" in an icy tone and swept on.

I nearly giggled but managed a courteous "Good morning" in reply.

"That's our First Floor Front," I told Max as we set off. "Think of the pleasure she will have in reporting my scandalous behavior to Mrs. Hall, on the off chance that that lady hasn't already caught the act from an upstairs window!"

9

Mrs. Lewis and her grandniece lived in a tiny hamlet with an unpronounceable name near Colwyn Bay on the north coast of Wales. Since this was my first visit to the area, Max had decided to take us through Shrewsbury and along a scenic route through narrow valleys between hills of intense green up toward the coast. Sometimes the road wound along beside wintry streams and then rose twisting to summits richly crowned with brown bracken and outcroppings of gray rock. Occasionally we passed the fragments of a ruined abbey or castle. We stopped for lunch in the charming little town of Ruthin and soon afterward reached the seaside. Since our appointment was for the following day, we drove on to our hotel, going past Colwyn Bay toward Llandudno to

Bodysgallen Hall, where Max had booked us for the two nights of our stay.

The hotel could not have been lovelier. A seventeenth-century house, handsomely appointed, it stood on a jewel-green hill surrounded by manicured gardens. I was shown to a delightful bedroom overlooking the countryside. Max's room was opposite. How tactful he was, I thought, to arrange separate rooms for us.

From the moment we arrived Max made me feel positively enveloped in admiration and affection. Throughout the delicious and leisurely dinner, and afterward making love, he conveyed his delight in our new relationship, and for my part I felt quite idiotically happy.

The next morning we found our two ladies, not in a rose-trellised cottage, as I had romantically imagined, but in one of a row of newly built stuccoed boxes filled with modern conveniences. The aged but sprightly Mrs. Lewis and her kindly middle-aged niece served us coffee and expressed mild surprise at my interest in the Marius Hart letters. Mrs. Lewis explained that she had nearly discarded them when the old house was given up, but "Father had always said they should be kept as Great-grandfather had been quite well-known in his day." Max pleased them with some anecdotes about Sir Cyril, and Mrs. Lewis readily gave her consent for us to make photocopies of the letters.

"There is also some music here if you would care to have a look at it," she added. I saw with excitement that the manuscript was titled "Nocturne" and dated 1858, the year of Hart's death. A brief look showed that this was a hitherto unpublished work, which promised to be a complex and richly developed piece.

Mrs. Lewis asked rather timidly if perhaps a library might wish to have the originals of the letters and the manuscript, and I promised to inquire at the British Library for her,

where I was sure the acquisition would be welcome. When
we had made our copies and returned with the materials, the
ladies said good-bye in a flurry of mutual thanks and promises that we would return.

"What darlings they are," I said to Max as we drove away.
"I was afraid after the first reply to my letter that there would
be problems." The niece had explained that "Aunt had been
very ill, poor dear," when my letter arrived but had pulled
through "in fine style."

While we were engaged in making the copies I had not
tried to read any of the spidery handwriting in the letters.
Like a child with a box of treasures, I waited until we returned to the hotel and settled into the deep chairs by the
window of my room with a set of copies for each of us.

There were ten letters written by Hart to his wife, Sarah,
over a four-month period in 1848, when Hart was at their
home in London while his wife paid a visit to her family in
Wales. When I saw the date 1848 my heart gave a leap, for
in that year Chopin had visited London, suffering from the
tuberculosis from which he died in the following year.

Could Hart have met Chopin? Quickly I skimmed through
the first few letters, and there it was. "Max! Look at this letter. He did—he met Chopin!"

Dearest Sarah,
I have seen him and heard him play! Never shall I forget
this incomparable evening. As you know, Monsieur Chopin
does not care to give public recitals and I had despaired of
hearing him at all. Imagine my joy when my pupil, Lady
Adelaide, obtained an entree for me to Lord Falmouth's,
where Chopin performed tonight.

He looks very pale—he is consumptive, as everyone
knows—but what refinement, what distinction in that no-
ble face. And his playing! Exactly as I imagined, he plays
with supreme delicacy but with underlying strength. There

*is nothing effete in his music or in his execution of it, yet it
is free of the crashing and banging which some of our
boorish virtuosi seem to regard as the ultimate in technique.*

*And now, Sarah, for the great climax of the evening for
me. Despite his exhaustion Chopin graciously spoke with
many of those present and I was fortunate enough to be
presented to him. Imagine my ecstasy when his pale face
broke into a smile as he pressed my hand and said that he
admired my work and was honored to meet me!*

"It's marvelous, darling," Max said. "This will add a touch
to your life of Marius Hart that will appeal to many readers,
not to music scholars alone."

Hart's other letters contained many references to domestic
matters and to the health of their infant son. Hart had married late and become a father for the first time at the age of
thirty-eight. Now he was anxious for the return to London of
Sarah and the child. There seemed to be no financial problems. He was much in demand as a concert performer and
evidently commanded top fees as a teacher. He and his wife
moved in distinguished social circles, and Hart's fame as a
composer was evidently extensive enough for Chopin, living
in France, to have known his work.

I thought of Patch's belief that artists are often neglected in
their lifetimes and reflected that this was a popular myth seldom borne out in fact. Here was Marius Hart, popular and
successful in his day. If he did not achieve the lasting fame of
a Chopin it was quite simply because he did not produce a
body of work of comparable genius. Fond as I was of Patch, I
could never believe that her Anton Lenski was destined for
belated fame. There had to be substantial achievement to become a star in the galaxy.

That afternoon Max and I drove into Llandudno for tea
and wandered into an antique shop, where I discovered a

marvelous bronze bust of Chopin, about twelve inches high, complete with its own pedestal. We were both amused at the coincidence of finding such an object on the very day of reading Hart's letter about the composer. I looked longingly at the bust but smiled when I saw the price, which was far beyond my budget. Instead I bought a little book for Max and he presented me with a charming little candle holder.

That evening at dinner Max surprised me by mentioning that he had recently told his wife it was time for them to think about being divorced, but that she had refused to consider it, making all sorts of objections he found unconvincing.

"But doesn't she want to be free to marry again?"

"Apparently not. She seems to like Horrid Hugh well enough as a sort of romantic Dobbin, but she evidently doesn't want to marry him." While Max did not say so explicitly, he seemed to imply that after being married to someone as scintillating as Max, Cynthia would find other prospects dull, even though their marriage had been in name only for some years.

How awfully conceited he is, I thought, looking at Max with amusement. Yet I could readily believe that his charm could be devastating to anyone who fell totally under its spell. I only hope it doesn't happen to me, I thought. But why is he telling me all this? Is he afraid that I may begin to expect a promise of marriage and is he preparing his defenses? Certainly the man whose wife refuses to grant him a divorce holds the time-honored position of being free to engage in romantic encounters without subsequent responsibility. I longed to tell him that he need have no fear on my account but of course I said nothing, simply floating with the current of pleasure in our holiday.

On the following morning we set off for London, and it

was on the last lap of our journey that we first talked about Alan. After lunch I drove for a while, and presently Max began speaking about the impressive sets for a production of *Don Giovanni* we had seen at Convent Garden before Christmas.

"Your son told me he is working in stage design," I said, hoping to elicit some sign of favorable interest.

"Hm. Yes. So he says." The hostility was chilling.

I took my eyes off the road for a moment to look at him. "Max, what is wrong between you and Alan?"

Long pause. "Well, if you must know . . . he prefers members of his own sex."

"So? Is that some sort of crime?"

Max sat forward, his eyes flashing in anger. "I might have known you would defend him, Jane. All you young people are the same. Anything is all right in today's world. Old-fashioned standards are antiquated and Victorian. I know the whole recital."

Oh, dear, I thought. Poor Max. And poor Alan. I was tempted to retort that Max himself was scarcely a model of old-fashioned virtues but I knew it was pointless. Instead, I tried a few comments along the lines of having tolerance toward individual differences, but Max merely became more agitated.

"After all," I added, "Alan is still young—not yet twenty-two. Perhaps this is a passing phase."

"That's what Cynthia says. But of course, she adores Alan and will always support him, whatever happens."

I was glad to know that at least Alan's mother did not share Max's antagonism. Then we dropped the subject and soon recaptured the sense of mutual pleasure that had marked our holiday.

1 0

Some two weeks after our return from Wales, I came home one day to find a heavy package awaiting me. It contained the bronze bust of Chopin that Max and I had seen in the antique shop in Llandudno. When Max came to call for me that evening he was as excited as a child at the success of his surprise. He told me he had phoned the owner of the shop from our hotel in Bodysgallen and directed her to send the bust to me in London.

"I was afraid you would refuse to accept it at the time, but now that it's here you can't send it back!"

I couldn't help laughing at his triumphant expression. "You win—I love it!"

That evening Max asked me to cover a pair of concerts for

him and write the review for his column. "I must run over to Paris on some family matters," he explained.

"Well," I said doubtfully, "I suppose I can do it, but it won't sound like your style. Shall I put my name or initials at the end of the copy when I send it in?"

"Oh, that's not necessary. Just say it's from me. You know my likes and dislikes by now. Simply follow my usual line."

"But Max, why don't you just omit this week's column? Surely they will understand?"

Max looked uncomfortable. "They're getting a bit touchy about that. Besides, these are things that really ought to be covered."

"Then isn't there someone on the staff who can do it?"

The mulish look of the spoiled child came over Max's face. "Look, Jane, if you don't want to do it, please say so."

I smiled—always the key to handling Max, as I was learning.

"Actually, I would love to do it. It would be fun." If deception was involved, I thought, it was his responsibility, not mine.

And in the end, I did enjoy doing the reviews.

The first event I covered was an all-Mozart concert given by the London Philharmonic Orchestra, under the baton of a distinguished Austrian in his late seventies. One could say nothing but good things about the beautifully controlled rendition, which allowed Mozart to shine through in all his perfection. It was a pleasure to pay homage to this great conductor and to the orchestra that responded so splendidly to his direction.

The second concert presented a minor challenge for me as surrogate reviewer. The program opened with a brief contemporary work in a vein similar to that of the Anton Lenski score about which Patch and I had so vigorously disagreed. Desperately I tried to listen with an open mind, but what I heard was chiefly a series of piercing shrieks alternating with booms of percussion, with no perceivable musical text.

I knew that Max felt as I did that this kind of music was a dead end and that the best music of the future would follow new paths within familiar tonalities. At the same time I had noticed that, although this was Max's private belief, he never expressed it openly in his column. Thus I began this review with a comment on the "enterprising" young composer whose work was "brief but pungent," deftly avoiding any real critical evaluation of the music.

When Max returned the following week I showed him my copy of the material I had sent to *Apollo* and was relieved when he expressed his delight with the reviews.

"Exactly what I should have said," he exclaimed, "and beautifully phrased. Thank you, darling!"

When Max glowed with enthusiasm he was irresistible, and I thought again how fortunate I was to have this charming man in my life.

About this time, some incidents occurred that proved to have a bearing on future events. One day early in February I had dropped in for lunch at the pleasant little buffet in the lower level of the National Gallery in Trafalgar Square. It was well after one o'clock and all the tables were taken. As I stood with my tray, looking for an empty chair, I saw Alan Fordham sitting with a bearded young man. Alan looked up at the same moment, smiled in recognition, and invited me to share their table.

"Jane—Winfield, is it? This is my friend Jeremy Welch."

I realized at once that this was Patch's Jeremy and that he did not remember me from our fleeting introduction at the bookshop some months earlier. Before I could reply, Alan startled me by bringing up the subject of his conflict with his father and assuming that I was his ally.

"Jane knows the whole story," he said to Jeremy. And to me, "I hear you are on my side, Jane. I appreciate your support."

"Your father told you that?"

"Yes. I don't think he much liked it, but I asked him straight out and he confessed."

From Alan's friendliness I could tell that he was fully aware of his parents' separate lives and accepted me as a friend of his father's without much caring about the nature of our relationship. And as the two young men talked to me about their difficulties in avoiding harassment, it was clear that they cared deeply for each other.

When they had gone, I sat sipping my tea and musing on the curious web of relationships I had chanced upon. Poor Patch, I thought. I wonder if she knows about Jeremy and Alan?

Within a week I had an answer to my question. Patch and I had gone to a performance of the Royal Ballet at the opera house in Covent Garden, where I had booked seats in the stalls circle, a ring of seats a few steps above the main floor. At the first interval we went down to the narrow curved foyer where elegantly dressed people chatted, ignoring the crush around them. We decided to get into the queue for coffee, as the bar looked hopelessly mobbed.

As I gazed about I suddenly found myself looking straight at Max, who stood not twenty feet away in a little group facing my way. Over the intervening heads I could see that he was with his family. Cynthia looked dazzling in a gown of such elegant simplicity that it could only be the product of a top designer. Sheila, on the other hand, was dressed in what might be called the requisite garb for the theatrical set—very expensive rags. When I had seen her at the Tate, she and her friend Fritz had both worn jeans and T-shirts. Now she wore a long dress of extremely wrinkled cotton and an open-weave baggy sweater hung with assorted chains, her beauty glowing above her garments like an exquisite flower blooming in an unweeded garden. Alan stood between his mother and sister, looking exceedingly handsome in conventional evening dress.

The four of them stood in a semicircle, listening attentively to a small man with his back to me, whose long gray locks brushing the collar of his green velvet coat proclaimed him a theatrical personage. Max's wife was an active patron of the Royal Ballet, and this was no doubt one of the rare occasions on which they made a public appearance together. In the brief moment in which I had seen the group, it was evident that neither Max nor Alan had seen me, and thinking it best to avoid a meeting, I turned to Patch to suggest that we abandon the coffee queue, which looked hopelessly long, and opt for a breath of fresh air instead. She agreed, and as we turned to go I saw her stare at the Fordham group and noticed a deep flush appear beneath her freckles.

So she does know about Jeremy and Alan, I thought. It must still be a painful association for her. How nice it would be if love affairs could be quickly forgotten. And I thought not only of Patch and Jeremy but of my own past infatuation with Brian, only now beginning to heal.

11

M y thoughts of Brian seemed to have conjured him out of the air, for the next day I received a letter from him that threatened to topple the little structure of stability I had created in my life. At the sight of his handwriting my heart began a sort of sickening *thud-thud*.

Dear Janie, the letter began. Oh, dear God. Don't let anything start again. Don't let me be hurt again. I read on:

They are giving me a fellowship for spring quarter. You remember that project I wanted to do on some Colonial settlers in upstate New York? Well, the big news is that I am coming over to England to look up the documents from that end and check out the backgrounds of my group before they

*left home. Of course I want to see you. It's all over with
Linda, by the way. Sorry about all that. Hope you are OK.
You know you'll always be my girl. All my love,*

Brian

Incredulously, I read his note over and over, shaking with
anger. The insolence of it. The casual reference to Linda,
the girl for whom he had broken off with me: *Sorry about all
that.* The assumption that of course I was meekly waiting for
him to come back.

With trembling hands, I snatched up pen and paper and
wrote:

*Brian, I don't want to see you. Please don't come here. If
you do, I shall leave London until you have gone.*

Hurriedly, I scrawled an envelope to the Connecticut address given in his letter, fumbled for an airmail stamp, and,
in my haste to leave the house, tripped over my boot and
pitched headlong to the floor, getting a nasty crack on my
elbow as I fell. Gasping, I tossed the boot across the room
and pulled myself up with my back against the faded chintz
sofa, cradling my arm and moaning in pain.

Tears began to pour down my face and I sat in a stupor,
not aware of weeping, simply watching with detached wonder
as the tears fell down the front of my blouse and soaked
through to the skin.

The summer before last came back to me as if it were
yesterday, the time I had tried to block out of my mind for so
long. It was August, and I had finally begun to mend after
the farewell phone call to Brian in February, in which he had
acknowledged that he was involved with a girl named Linda.
It was a Friday afternoon and I was at home alone, lying in
the sun in the back garden reading a novel, when Brian ar-

rived at the door. He swept me into his arms, and it suddenly seemed as if he had never gone away, as if the nightmare of the past six months had evaporated into nothing. He told me things were all off with Linda; it had been a mistake. He still loved me. Would I forgive him?

Of course I would. I felt nothing but an overwhelming joy. Brian was here. He was mine again. A thousand Lindas were nothing to me now.

He had the key to a friend's cabin in the mountains near Lake Arrowhead.

"You remember Steve? He said I can have the place for a week. Come on, Janie, let's go."

I hastily packed a bag, canceled a lunch date with a girlfriend, left a note for my father, and went off with Brian in a daze of happiness so acute it was akin to pain.

The week we spent together was glorious. It was like falling in love again. We talked about the future and it was agreed that if Brian was given a promise of tenure, as he expected, I would go to Connecticut at the end of the year and continue work on my dissertation there.

When Brian had been back in Connecticut for about a month, I realized one evening that I hadn't heard from him in over a week. It was after eleven o'clock, when the telephone rates were lower, and I decided on an impulse to dial his number. The moment he answered I knew he was not alone.

"Is someone there?" I asked.

"Oh, well, yes. Just a friend." His embarrassment was so obvious that I took the plunge before I had time to think.

"Brian, is it Linda?"

"Look, I can't talk now. I'll call you back later, OK?"

I hung up, feeling utterly numb. Half an hour later Brian called, full of apologies, glibly blaming himself for his inconstancy. He cared for both of us—what could he do? He had really thought it was all over with Linda, but she had begged him to try again. I let him go on until he stopped. Then I said quite simply that this was the end for me. No matter what happened in the future, we would never see each other again.

That was when the icy coldness invaded my being. I felt no panic, no hysterical desire to weep. I sat for hours staring into space.

Now, sitting on the floor in my room in London, I wept helplessly, as I had never done before, reliving what I had for so long shut away. One betrayal I might have accepted, but the second was unbearable. How different it would have been if Brian had been true, if we had found a fulfilling life together. On and on I wept, until utter exhaustion drained away the last of the tears.

Wearily I tore up the note to Brian, realizing that its desperate tone would seem like a challenge to him. Instead I wrote a mild letter saying that I was extremely busy and that perhaps it would be better for us not to see each other. I added a few clichés about time passing and water under the bridge and so forth. Brian may have been brilliant in his field, but in his personal life his vocabulary was at the level of soap opera. Privately I resolved that if he did turn up I would disappear from London at once, but it was no use telling him that in advance.

The next day after receiving Brian's letter I wandered about feeling utterly depressed and unable to concentrate on my work. In the late afternoon I walked along to the post office in Theobalds Road, looked idly into shop windows without seeing what was there, crossed the road for no apparent reason, and found myself walking through the gate into Gray's Inn and down the long walk to James's office. The receptionist smiled at me.

"You'll be wanting Mr. Hall, I expect. I am afraid he is

out, but he may return within the hour if you would care to wait."

I thanked her and wandered disconsolately back along the walk. Why did I want to see James? Surely I wasn't planning to cry on his shoulder, tempting though it would be. Suddenly I looked up and there he was coming toward me, his face beaming.

"Jane! How good to see you! Come and have some tea."

I hesitated, feeling that I was not up to bright conversation.

James looked at me more closely and instantly took charge. "What you need is a drink, my girl. This way, please." He swept me back toward his office, chatting away about the case on which he had just appeared in court. Once in his office, he lit the fire, settled me in a chair, and took two glasses from a small cabinet.

"I prescribe a whisky. Soda?"

"Yes, please."

He handed me the drink, took his own glass, and sat down in the adjoining chair, his clear blue eyes looking at me with concern.

"Now, sip or talk, just as you like."

I took a large gulp of my drink and sank back in the chair, feeling the sheer comfort of James's presence.

"I *was* feeling dreadful but I didn't know it showed."

"Oh, dear, yes. I knew something was wrong. You usually have such a—how can I describe it?—a sort of sparkle."

Astonished but pleased at this description of myself, I smiled.

"You see, there it is!" James looked as delighted as a parent whose child has just shown to good advantage.

Suddenly it seemed all right to tell James my problem. "You see, I had a letter from someone I used to care for. He may be coming to London and I can't bear to see him."

James was silent, almost in a reverie. "Yes," he said at last, "I think I understand. It's difficult, isn't it?"

He paused, then seemed to decide to go on.

"Quite recently I saw someone who had once meant a great deal to me, until she broke it off. I simply saw her on the street and I went about feeling awful for days."

Silly girl, I thought, not to appreciate James.

We smiled at each other and went on to talk of other things. Afterward I remembered that James had said not a word to me about Max, although he must have known I was seeing someone. His mother and Miss Leach undoubtedly recorded Max's comings and goings, and it was inevitable that Mrs. Hall had described me in the classic British phrase as being "no better than she should be." Since Max never stayed overnight and spent only an occasional afternoon or evening in my room, she could not technically object to his presence, but I was sure she would have lost no opportunity to warn James against this Jezebel on the premises.

1 2

G radually the effect of Brian's letter subsided and I began to feel more cheerful. If he did come to London it would be some weeks off, and I decided to cope when the time came. The cold of February brought a damp and penetrating chill that kept me bundled up outdoors but was invigorating if I walked briskly enough. My work on Marius Hart was beginning to take shape, and I was feeling comfortable with my life again.

The only source of uneasiness was the news that a new Jack the Ripper was stalking the London streets. For the third time in two months the body of a young woman had been found strangled, the last one in Regent's Park. The police were now certain that the crimes were committed by the same man, although the locations varied, the first body having been found near Liverpool Street Station and the second on the Embankment. I carefully avoided walking alone at night and took more taxis than I could afford.

One day I was returning to my room about half past four in the afternoon when to my surprise I saw Alan Fordham step out of a small car that was parked in the lane.

"Hello, Jane. I was hoping you would turn up."

"Alan! Come in and have a cup of tea."

"I'd love it, thanks."

I plugged in the electric teakettle and set out a tray.

"How on earth did you know where I live?"

"Simple enough. I lifted your address from Father's book. I hope you don't mind."

I realized that Alan's voice was shaking slightly. In a moment we settled down with our tea and he began.

"Jane, I need to talk to you. Father seems to have gone bonkers about this whole business. You will never believe this, but he says he will cut off my allowance unless I stop seeing Jeremy, and I have to have regular sessions with a psychiatrist to be *cured*. As if I have some *disease*. It's too absolutely Victorian."

"I'm so sorry, Alan."

"The money is actually from Grandfather," Alan went on. Apparently Sir Cyril had left a fairly large sum in trust for both children, but Max retained control until each reached the age of twenty-five.

"Poor old Jeremy hasn't a bean. The only thing I can do is get a job, and I am fit for nothing. I'm just getting a toehold in theater design, and of course that will be all off. I don't mind working, honestly, but it seems so beastly unfair when the money is actually there, going begging. Will you talk to him about it, Jane?"

"I can try. But he didn't respond very well when the subject came up the last time. I'm afraid it won't help. What about your mother?"

"Mother's marvelous. She says she will help me out as much as she can, but he has her in rather the same bind. She has only a little money of her own, and Father has threatened her with extinction if she does anything for me in a big way. At least I have her sympathy, which is more than I get from my sister."

"Does Sheila disapprove, then?"

"Oh, she doesn't care in the least what I do. It's simply that she adores Divine Daddy and takes his part in everything."

I noted with amusement that much as Alan detested his father at the moment, he had picked up Max's penchant for the epithet.

"Sheila can be so dim. She blames Mother for everything and thinks Daddy is next to a saint. The child is nineteen and I decided she should begin to face reality, so I told her about you and she simply refused to believe it. You see, I had never told her about the other—" Alan broke off, looking exceedingly embarrassed.

I smiled. "Don't worry. I have never imagined that I was the first woman in Max's life. But I am sorry if your sister is upset."

"Oh, she'll be all right. The odd thing is, she seems to be totally naive about sex. Most girls her age know plenty, but Sheila goes around like the girl in the Virgin Spring."

This confirmed the conversation I had heard between Sheila and Fritz at the Tate, but I could hardly tell Alan about that.

Alan stayed for over an hour, talking earnestly about his dilemma. He was desperately angry with Max, the kind of anger that builds slowly in someone of Alan's usually gentle nature. Although I protested again that I would have little influence with Max, I promised to do what I could.

"He admires you, Jane. He thinks you are terribly intelligent and also very sensible."

"Good heavens! Did he tell you all that?"

"Yes, quite seriously."

When Alan had gone I sat musing about Max's attitude and wondering how much of this opposition to Alan was simply a matter of Max's obsession with having his own way.

In the following week Max asked me if I would mind changing a date we had made for lunch the next day. "Someone I haven't seen for ages rang up and I didn't like to say no," he explained. His eyes were shining and a self-satisfied smile played over his face. I was sure that the "someone" was female, but I asked nothing and assured him that the change was quite all right.

That same day I had had a letter from Dr. Andrew Quentin, the professor who was directing my dissertation, saying that he expected to be in London for some time and asking me to let him know when I was free. I had written to him occasionally to report my progress on Marius Hart and had received encouraging replies. Now I called him at the friend's flat where he was staying.

"Jane! How are you?" The sound of the American voice gave me a slight tremor of homesickness. "Why don't we meet somewhere for tea today? We can have an informal chat and do a full-scale conference later on."

We agreed to meet at the Savoy. I took the bus down to the Strand and walked along toward the little street leading to the grand old hotel. The circular drive was crowded with taxis and limousines through which I picked my way to the entrance. Inside, I walked through the lobby and down the wide stairs to the lounge where tea was served in the afternoons. Beyond was the elegant restaurant overlooking the river, where I could see people lingering over their late luncheons.

At one of the tables along the wall I saw Dr. Quentin get up from his chair and greet me with a radiant smile. He was that rare creature, a good-looking man who seems to be unaware of his attractiveness. I had seen women students make their admiration pretty obvious and be greeted with modest courtesy and nothing more.

Watching me take off my cap, muffler, wool gloves, and coat, he asked if the cold weather bothered me. "It was like summer when I left Los Angeles the other day."

I assured him that I enjoyed being in London so much that nothing could detract from its charms.

"I love it too," he said fervently. "I suppose it was rather frivolous to meet here at the Savoy, but I've always liked the old place."

Settled into the charming little sofa beside Dr. Quentin's chair, I looked at him and thought with surprise, He's much younger than Max! I had always thought of him vaguely as "older" without any point of reference. Now I saw that although his brown hair was thinning at the top, he was probably only in his early thirties. Max was so lively that he seemed more youthful than he was, whereas Dr. Quentin had an air of reserve and a quiet dignity, which added years to his age. More than that, I saw again that fleeting look of pain which crossed his face at odd moments, causing him to retreat momentarily into a private world of his own.

It must be nearly three years now, I thought, since he lost his wife. What a charming girl she was. And a talented painter, just beginning her career. Dr. Quentin had invited the graduate students in my seminar to his home and I remembered her—the piquant face, the dark curly hair— laughing with us over her paint-stained fingers as she served us cake and coffee. Only two months later she was dead, struck by a car as she crossed the street. He had finished the term and carried on with his life, outwardly composed but clearly devastated. Two years ago, uncertain whether or not to ask him to direct my dissertation, I had consulted with the department chair. She told me he welcomed work that interested him and to go ahead and ask. In fact, Dr. Quentin liked my proposal on Marius Hart, and now he listened with interest to my account of my current activities.

"I'm pleased that you found some of Hart's letters. Had you been to Wales before?"

"No, my first time. It's lovely, even in winter."

"Yes, I imagine so. I've been there only in the summer. Did you drive?"

I hesitated only for a moment. "Yes. A friend drove me there, Maxwell Fordham. He does music reviews for *Apollo* magazine."

"Any relation to Sir Cyril Fordham?"

"His son."

"I see. The son must be quite an old gentleman by now, isn't he?"

I smiled and could feel myself blushing. Shades of Patch, I thought. "No, he's in his forties. Sir Cyril was quite old when Max was born."

Dr. Quentin gave no sign of noticing my awkwardness and went serenely on. "I'll be most interested to see your copies of Hart's letters."

We talked on, drinking endless cups of tea and munching the delicious food from the tiered cake server. I noticed his long slender fingers and looked down at my own small hands. "You have musician's hands. I envy you that. Even if I had wanted a concert career in piano, which thank heaven I didn't, I could never have made it with these."

He smiled. "Yes, my teachers were forever telling me how

lucky I was to have the right hands. But I'm with you. The performer leads a terrible life. I much prefer the life I have now."

I told him about Patch. "She's the right sort of person for performance. The cello is her whole life and she couldn't imagine doing anything else."

The pianist in the center of the lounge had begun with the usual teatime music, interspersed with a bit of Chopin, at which we exchanged a smile. I looked with pleasure at the marble pillars, the paintings on the walls, and the old-fashioned elegance, which had happily not been redone in chrome and glass. I remembered Max's remark one day that "no one goes to the Savoy anymore," meaning that it was out of favor with his particular set.

"I used to go there often," he had said, with a dreamy-eyed look, suggesting romantic assignations with some favored lady. "But where can one go today?" He sounded like one of those plaintive letters to the *Times* about how London has changed. "The Arabs own the Dorchester, and the last time I was in the Savoy it was absolutely filled with rich Americans. Oh, sorry, Jane—but you do know what I mean!"

Thus I was surprised to see Max himself stepping out of the dining room and even more surprised to see that the lady with him was Lady Muriel Dodson. They had obviously just finished a late lunch and were walking through the lounge, both looking serious. Suddenly they stopped and stood facing each other. I could hear nothing of their conversation over the sound of the piano music and the murmur of voices, but I could see the intensity of her expression as she spoke to him. He nodded in what appeared to be assent and they stood for a moment longer, oblivious to their surroundings, before turning to go.

This was the day for which Max had changed our lunch date. So the invitation must have come from Lady Muriel—

"someone I haven't seen for a long time." I was fairly sure that there had been some sort of affair between them after Patch's father died, but I would not have expected Lady Muriel to renew the relationship now, after several years of apparent contentment in her marriage to Dods. So the Savoy was a familiar place of rendezvous for them in the past. How sad for everyone, I thought, if this is more than a passing thing.

At that moment I noticed a man holding a newspaper get up from a chair along the wall to my left. It was Lord Dodson, and it was plain that he had seen exactly what I had seen. His hands clenched until the newspaper crumpled. After a moment he dropped the paper on the chair, tossed some money on the table, and strode toward the lobby in the wake of Max and Lady Muriel.

My heart contracted with pity for him, knowing how he adored his wife. He must have followed her here, at who knows what cost to his pride. Would he tell his wife what he had seen? Or would he wait and hope that it would pass? I knew that Max would have no compunction about renewing an affair with Lady Muriel. Self-sacrifice was not his style. I could only hope that Lady Muriel wouldn't fall under his spell.

Dr. Quentin saw plainly that I was distressed.

"Are you all right?" he asked.

I told him in a few sentences who the people were and what I had seen.

He looked thoughtful. "I see that Mr. Fordham is a most attractive man. Are you in love with him, Jane?" So he had after all noticed my confusion earlier. It was obvious that his question was asked with real concern for me.

"No," I said. "I'm very fond of him and I do enjoy his company, but that's all."

"Then your concern is more for your friend and her family than for yourself?"

"Oh, yes! Patch adores her mother and she is extremely fond of her stepfather. It would be devastating for all of them if—if—"

"Will you tell your friend about this?"

"Tell Patch? Oh, no! It may mean nothing after all."

Then we turned the conversation to other things. He told me briefly about the work he was doing that had brought him to London during his current leave from the university.

"I'll be in and out of London for several weeks," he said, and we set a date for a conference on my progress on Marius Hart.

13

W hen I saw Max the next evening he was in high spirits. We stopped for drinks after attending a concert at the Royal Festival Hall, and Max became archly sentimental about this having been the place of our first meeting.

"You and your wretched book," he teased. "I wanted to talk to you from the first moment when I picked up your program from the floor and you gave me that cool little look of yours. You weren't flirting—you simply were not interested."

This was not the first time I was aware of how much Max had felt challenged initially by my indifference to his charms. Even now, when we were occasionally intimate, he knew quite well that I was not passionately in love with him. This must have been something of a novelty for him. I thought of Lady Muriel and realized that I felt not a trace of jealousy, only a fervent hope, as I had told Dr. Quentin the day before, that for her own sake she would refrain from becoming involved with Max again.

I had been waiting for an opportunity to bring up the subject of Alan, as I had promised to do, when Max suddenly plunged into the matter himself.

"I understand my son has been making a nuisance of himself." He looked at me accusingly.

"Not at all. I was happy to see him."

"I suppose he has been weeping on your shoulder and saying how unreasonable I am."

"But Max, dear, don't you think you *are* being a bit unreasonable? Such extreme measures as you propose will only make him bitter against you."

"I don't give a damn if he is bitter against me. I simply want this nonsense to stop."

As I had done before, in our first talk about Alan on the drive home from Wales, I tried gently to urge him to take a milder view, but he was adamant. Whatever influence Alan may have thought I would have with Max was certainly not apparent, and I was forced to abandon any further effort to change his mind.

Max's parting shot had all the air of finality. "I have given him a deadline to make up his mind whether or not to cooperate. Sometime next month I must go to Paris again on business, and when I return he either accedes to my demands or he gets no more money!"

One evening toward the end of February Max was again extremely upset, but this time it concerned not Alan but Sheila. We had gone to the Ivy for a supper after the theater, and I had sensed all evening that Max was perturbed.

"Jane, do you mind if I'm an awful bore and talk about something that's bothering me?"

"No, of course not. What is it?"

"Sheila has done the most extraordinary thing. You remember that she went to New York twice with Frightful Fritz for screen tests and whatnot? He wanted her to go again this week—why all these trips I'm sure I don't know—but since our friends the Caswells are not in New York at the moment, I told her absolutely she could not go. We had rather a flaming row about it last night, and today she simply went off with him to New York, leaving a note giving the name of the hotel where they are stopping."

I looked at Max and saw the bewilderment in his face. Unlike the anger he displayed toward Alan, his reaction to Sheila's defection was one of hurt. To think that his darling, his pet, could defy him filled him with pain.

"I'm not much of a success as a father, it seems. What in heaven's name does one do?"

"Has she been troublesome before?"

"No, never! That is to say, she has always been a bit headstrong and I suppose she does rather like having her own way about things—doesn't everyone? But she has always been such a dear little thing."

I was tempted to say that a girl of nineteen who has been indulged all her life is quite likely from here on to do exactly as she pleases, regardless of the wishes of her doting father, but this hardly seemed an appropriate response. Poor Max! I tried a few consoling statements and was astonished to see that, unlike his opposition to anything I said about Alan, he seized eagerly on any hopeful remarks about Sheila.

"They will be back in two days," Max went on. "It's as well that Cynthia is out of town. I think my best course is to be quite calm when Sheila returns and try talking to her reasonably. Do you agree?"

"Yes, absolutely." Too bad, I thought, that you can't apply that approach to Alan.

A few days later, Alan rang me up and asked me to meet him for drinks. When we were settled at a small table in the wine bar, I could only report my total failure to influence Max in his favor.

"I suppose he told you about his famous deadline?"

"Yes."

"He has made an appointment for me to see his shrink—some old pal from his Cambridge days—for the week after he comes back from Paris. By the bye, did he tell you about Sheila and the mad dash to New York?"

"Yes. He was most unhappy about it."

"Of course she told him they had separate rooms at the hotel and he believed her."

I had wondered at Max's lack of concern over that aspect of her escapade. Now I understood.

"The odd thing is," Alan went on, "that a month ago I would have believed her myself, but all that is changed now, only Father hasn't noticed a thing. It must have been three weeks ago that the bell rang for little sister. She suddenly began going about looking starry-eyed and dazed and being discovered in passionate embraces with Fritz. One kept tripping over them all about the house—except when Father was at home, when they simply made a rapid exit and disappeared, no doubt to Fritz's place."

"I am sure Max knows nothing about it. He was disturbed enough that your sister would defy him. I can imagine how he would feel about this!"

"What puzzles me, Jane, is that when Sheila first came home the other night, she was laughing and defiant. Father was amazingly patient with her. I expected him to do the paternal rage bit, but instead he went in for 'more in sorrow than in anger.' It must have worked because the child has been acting positively subdued ever since. The thing is, though, that it was not until the next morning that I noticed the change in her. She acts frightened."

"Surely not of Max?"

"That's just it. It couldn't be that, could it? And yet, in some indescribable way, she looks to me as if under all the bravado she is scared to death. I admit I'm a bit worried about her. Spoilt though she is, I'm fond of the brat."

How ironic, I thought, that all of Max's devotion went to the willful Sheila while Alan's good qualities remained unappreciated.

14

One evening early in March Max asked me to cover another concert for him on Wednesday of the following week.

"I'm leaving for Paris on Monday, you know, and not returning until Thursday."

"But Max, I'm going to Birmingham on Wednesday and Thursday."

"Oh, blast, I forgot. Can't you change the days?"

"No," I said firmly, but with a smile, "I can't." I had booked a hotel for Wednesday night in Birmingham near the university, where I needed to look at some materials in the library, and I had no intention of catering to Max's whims.

Moreover, I was glad of the legitimate excuse, as I felt uncomfortable about doing his column a second time.

"I daresay I'll find someone else to do it," Max said sulkily. Presently, however, he forgot his pique and we spent a pleasant evening together.

Although the papers I examined in Birmingham the following week did not prove to be especially useful, I enjoyed getting out of London and seeing a little of the countryside between the two great cities. Coming back on the train on Thursday afternoon I read a newspaper account of another victim of the London killer and shivered when I saw that this time the body had been found on the east side, not more than a mile or so from where I lived. I was glad that it would still be daylight when I arrived in London. I could take the tube to Russell Square and walk safely home from there.

It was not yet five o'clock when I emerged from the tube station and saw to my dismay that patches of fog were drifting along the sidewalk. I walked briskly along Guilford Street, hoping that the fog would clear. Instead, it perversely began to thicken. As I approached Lamb's Conduit Street I realized that I could scarcely distinguish the street name on the corner of the building.

That was when I noticed the footsteps behind me. Certainly there was nothing unusual about people walking in the streets of London. What struck me as odd was that when I paused to look up at the street sign, the steps behind me paused too. It was too early for the surge of office workers whose day ended at five. At the moment the street seemed to be deserted except for me and the person behind me.

I hurried on toward my turning in Doughty Street. Surely, I thought, he will go straight on. But when I turned to the right at the corner I soon realized that the heavy tread was still there. The fog seemed thicker than ever here, where the street was less brightly lighted than in Guilford Street. I be-

gan to fumble in my handbag for my keys, tripped, and
nearly fell. The footsteps paused again. My heart began to
thud achingly and my breath came in little gasps. I had never
experienced abject terror before, and I was horrified at how
incapable I felt of thinking clearly. I could picture myself
opening the gate in the lane and trying to unlock the door to
my room. In the dark and narrow area by my entrance I
could easily be overpowered and no one would see or hear.

Instinctively I began to run. It wasn't far now. If only I
could reach the house! Suddenly my paralyzed brain began
to function. I needn't turn into the lane at all. I could go to
the front door, where at least I would be visible from the
street. Would an assailant follow me there?

I fled past the remaining houses and reached desperately
for the front gate, somehow managing to open the latch on
the first try. Slamming the gate behind me, I ran frantically
up the walk and simply threw myself against the heavy door,
pressing the bell and banging with my fists, crying out
"Help!" in what sounded to my own ears as a faint and feeble
voice. I turned then to look back and saw the shadowy figure
of a man, obscured by the fog, standing beyond the gate staring at me. My keys were in my hand, and as I tore off my
glove and tried to find the lock with my shaking hand, the
door opened and there, blissfully, stood James.

As I stumbled into the house I looked once more and saw
the man still staring. It seemed in that fleeting moment that
he looked familiar, but the fog was too thick to see anything
but a nebulous blur.

"Jane, what is it?" James put out a hand toward me and I
simply threw myself into his arms, gasping out my fear and
my relief. He reached out to close the door and then his arms
went around me again and he held me firmly, as one would
hold a terrified child.

"It's all right," he murmured soothingly. "It's all right now."

"Oh, James, I'm so glad you're here."

Then I turned my head and saw Mrs. Hall standing in the passage staring. Her first look of astonishment changed to a glare of animosity that made me shrink as if I had been struck.

"What's going on?" she asked freezingly.

James explained what had happened, at which she gave a snort of disdain and retreated to her sitting room.

James came with me into my room to see me settled. It was the first time, I realized, that he had been there. The table lamp was already alight, since I had set the timer early enough so that it would always be on when I returned. Now James opened the outside door and peered over the side gate and up and down the lane.

"No one about," he reported, coming back in and turning the lock and deadbolt from the inside.

"Window seems secure," he added, confirming that it was locked and closing the curtains again after his inspection.

"I'm really fine now," I said shakily. "Thank you so much. I feel like an idiot."

James turned to look at me with an expression of such concern that I could feel tears pricking my eyes. "It's not in the least idiotic. You must be extremely careful. Promise?"

I nodded.

When James had gone, I gathered up my bath things and started up the stairs. Suddenly I heard Mrs. Hall's voice through the open door of her sitting room.

"I did not know," she was saying, "that you and Miss Winfield were on intimate terms." I stood frozen at the foot of the steps.

"Well, hardly that, Mother."

"You seem to be well acquainted. Really, James—" At this

point the door closed abruptly and I could hear only her angry voice and James's low murmurs as I went up the stairs.

Poor James. Lying in the deliciously hot bath I reflected on his kindness and wondered how he could be so patient with his termagant mother.

Max was to call for me at seven, and I was glad not to face the evening alone. I decided to wear my favorite dress, a flame-colored silk I had chosen because it matched the gala elephants on the scarf Max had given me at Christmas. When he arrived I saw at once that he was preoccupied. I poured out the story of my fright at being followed and realized that he was scarcely listening. I felt a surge of anger at his indifference, but I knew Max well enough by now to know that any protest would be futile. Thank heaven, I thought for the hundredth time, that by some miracle I had escaped caring deeply for Max. As it was, I could find him irritating without being hurt by him. I paused in my story and knew that he was simply waiting for me to finish so that he could speak. Seizing his opportunity, he broke out at once.

"You are not the only one whose life was threatened this evening." The petulant look about his mouth intensified.

"What on earth?"

"My son Alan did me the kindness of informing me that he would see me dead before he would comply with my wishes."

"Alan said that?"

"Yes. With his arm raised in a most threatening attitude."

"Oh, Max, I'm so sorry. But wouldn't it be better to let him go his own way without opposition and see if it doesn't all come right in the end?"

"No, it's gone too far. I refuse to give in to threats of physical violence. He knows that the trust would terminate at my death. He actually rang up the family solicitor and asked him."

"But Max, you know that Alan would never do anything like that. Nevertheless, it should make you realize how strongly he feels about this."

We talked on in the same vein for a time, but when I saw that continued argument would accomplish nothing, I dropped the subject. We went to dinner at a restaurant we both liked, chatting amiably about other things. He expressed his delight that Sheila was "behaving like an angel." I told him briefly about my excursion to Birmingham, and he spoke of his recent trip to Paris.

Afterward I was happy to remember that the evening ended so pleasantly, for it was the last time I saw Max alive.

15

The next day was the fourteenth of March—the fateful date with which this story began. I had been working at the University of London Library, where I first met Patch going down in the lift. This was the day Patch and her parents were leaving for the Continent, they on their way to Italy for a few weeks and Patch to tour France and Germany with a chamber music group. I wondered if Dods had planned the trip to Italy to remove Lady Muriel from London, or if perhaps she herself wanted to escape from possible temptation.

Patch had been tremendously excited at winning the competition for a place as cellist with the group, and I was delighted for her. Because of my trip to Birmingham I had thought that I would not see her to say good-bye, but now I decided to drop in at Charlotte Street in case she had not gone yet. It was about half past three when I rang her bell and received no answer. At that moment the Gorgon appeared at the street door and greeted me.

"I'm afraid Miss Crawford has gone. She left in a taxi some time ago. So difficult to travel with that large cello case, isn't it? But such a splendid opportunity for her, I'm sure."

Patch had told me that ever since the day a letter had come for her addressed to "The Hon. Patricia Crawford," the Gorgon's hostility had changed to a dreadful fawning and an intolerable habit of inquiring after the health of Lady Muriel, whose identity she had pried from a reluctant Patch.

I walked back toward the Tottenham Court Road, idly wandering in and out of the shops, stopped for a coffee at a self-service bar, and went along Great Russell Street, where I browsed in a bookshop for a while. It was after four o'clock when I decided that I would treat myself to a taxi after my fright of the evening before, but such is the perversity of the London weather that the light rain which had been falling all afternoon had become a vigorous downpour and within minutes all the vacant taxis disappeared. I put up my umbrella, tied on the elephant scarf which I found in my coat pocket from the night before, and walked on toward Bloomsbury Square, where I could take a bus if no taxi turned up.

As I waited at the bus stop, dozens of taxis went by but all were taken. At last a Number 38 bus came and I stepped on, not really worried because it was still daylight. On the night before it was the thickening fog that had caused my terror; the rain held no such threat.

By the time I reached my stop in Theobalds Road and turned into John Street, as Doughty Street is called at that end, the rain had stopped. It was still not dark, and I felt no alarm as I walked down the long street, turned into the lane, and opened the gate to my side door. The usual fumble in my handbag did not produce my keys, and finally I took off my gloves and resorted to lifting out the contents item by item, laying them on the small brick step in front of the door. Still no keys. Exasperated with myself and wondering where on earth I had left them, I bent over and gathered up the assorted contents of my bag, stuffing everything back helter-skelter.

I'll have to go around to the front, I thought, dreading to face Mrs. Hall. Perhaps James would be home, as he was yesterday. I looked at my watch. Twenty minutes to five. Not very likely.

Before turning to go, I reached for the doorknob and gave it a turn, knowing it was useless because the lock was set to snap automatically when the door was closed. To my amazement the knob turned, and I opened the door and went in. The lamp was on, the faithful timer having done its work.

As I pulled off my scarf and put down my things I turned and saw beyond the coffee table a man's foot. Instantly I thought the man who had followed me the evening before had somehow gained access to my room, and I gasped and turned to run. But in the same moment I realized that the man was lying on the floor and that the foot was motionless and turned at an odd angle.

I took one terrified step forward and saw that it was Max. His body was bent at the waist, his head lying between the small table and the sofa. One arm was flung out and a crumpled paper was clutched in his hand. I rushed around the end of the table, stumbling over an object that proved to be my bronze bust of Chopin. Hastily I picked it up, thrust it out of the way, and knelt beside Max. I saw then there was an ugly mark on the side of his head near the temple and a smear of blood on his cheek.

"Max, Max!" I cried, shaking his shoulders. His face was utterly white, and the moment I touched his body I knew something was terribly wrong. Could he be simply unconscious? I must get help.

I staggered to my feet, my heart pounding and thumping painfully, and burst into the passage, calling out, "Mrs. Hall! Someone! Please help!"

I banged on the sitting-room door but no Mrs. Hall. Rushing back toward the telephone on the wall under the stairs, I was just preparing to ring the 999 emergency number when Mrs. Hall appeared at the foot of the stairs.

"What is the trouble now?" she asked testily. It was only afterward that I realized the absurdity of my crying out for help on two successive evenings.

"There's been an accident. I must get a doctor or an ambulance."

Mrs. Hall looked through the open door to my room and immediately went to Max and knelt beside him. Crisply she placed a hand over his wrist, raised one of his eyelids, and turned to stare at me with a look of loathing that made me shudder.

"This man is dead," she said. "As I am sure you very well know."

"No, I didn't know. I've never seen—I mean, I thought he might be unconscious—"

Ignoring me utterly, Mrs. Hall swept past me to the telephone and dialed. Incredulous, I heard her say, "I want the police. A man has been murdered!"

16

The next few hours marked the beginning of a nightmare time for me. As Mrs. Hall hung up the phone, Miss Leach appeared from the floor above and the two women retreated down the passage, talking in low voices and casting baleful glances at me. Stunned, I sat in a chair opposite the door to my room. Within minutes after the phone call two uniformed police officers arrived. Quietly they examined Max's body. Then one stationed himself at the door to my room while the other reported to the police station that there was indeed a dead man on the premises and that there were indications of foul play. A few minutes later two plainclothes officers arrived, followed by a steady stream of

technicians—photographer, fingerprint man, and so on—
and a doctor who officially pronounced Max to be dead.

The elder of the plainclothes officers spoke to us first. "I
am Detective Chief Inspector Kent and this is Detective Sergeant Wilson. May I ask all of you to remain here, please. I
shall need statements presently from everyone on the premises." When they had spent some time in my room, where I
could hear Inspector Kent talking with the technicians, both
officers returned to where we waited in the passage.

"Can someone please tell me the name of the deceased?"
asked the Inspector. I opened my lips to reply when, to my
astonishment, I heard Mrs. Hall say, in her crisp tone, "Yes.
His name was Maxwell Fordham." The Inspector evidently
saw my start of surprise and turned to me. "Is that correct,
miss?"

"Yes, it is," was all I could say.

The Inspector went on. "May I ask who placed the call for
the police?"

"I did." Mrs. Hall's lips were compressed.

"Thank you. And is there a room which we may have at
our disposal?" He looked inquiringly along the passage. Mrs.
Hall showed him her sitting room at the front of the house,
the dining room next to it, and the kitchen at the back. The
Inspector placed me in the dining room, with a uniformed
officer standing by, while he and the sergeant went into the
sitting room with Mrs. Hall, asking Miss Leach to wait. I
could hear the murmur of their voices without distinguishing
what was being said. Then the door opened and I heard the
Sergeant ask Miss Leach to please step in. What could Miss
Leach possibly have to say? I was soon to find out.

Meanwhile I sat in a kind of stupor. It was impossible that
Max should be dead. What could have happened? Did he
fall and strike his head? What was there in my room that
could inflict a fatal blow? And how did he get into my room

in the first place? If I had forgotten my keys, the door would still have been locked from the outside. My head began to ache with the effort of trying to puzzle it out.

When at last the Inspector came into the dining room he asked me to describe what had happened that afternoon. For the first of so many times to come, I recounted coming back to my room, looking for my keys, finding the door unlocked, and seeing Max's body on the floor.

"At what time did this occur?"

"I believe it was about twenty minutes to five."

"Can you tell us how Mr. Fordham gained entrance to your room? Did he have a key of his own?"

"No, he didn't have a key. I don't know how he came to be there. I'm sure that I locked the door when I went out."

"Sergeant, may I have the keys, please?" In a moment the sergeant returned, holding up a ring of keys on a pen so as not to touch them.

"Are these your keys, miss? They were lying on the table in your room."

"Yes, they are mine. I must have left them when I went out."

"And at what time did you leave the house today?"

"About eleven o'clock this morning."

"And will you please describe your movements during the remainder of the day?"

"Yes. I went to the library at the University of London at Russell Square. I did not go out for lunch, since I had had a late breakfast. About half past three I went to see a friend in Charlotte Street but she was not at home." Then I described how I had spoken with the Gorgon, had dawdled about in the shops, had coffee, browsed in a bookshop, and finally taken a bus to the stop in Theobalds Road, arriving at my room after half past four.

Inspector Kent looked at me gravely. "Miss Winfield, we

have witnesses who tell a very different story to the one you
have just given. I must caution you at this time that you have
the right to have a solicitor present and that any statements
you make may be taken down and used in evidence against
you. Do you wish to answer any further questions at this
time?"

Astonished, I replied at once, "Of course I do. I have no
idea what you mean. I have told you exactly what happened
today."

"Very well then. Please think carefully before you answer.
Did you return to this house today and were you in your
room at approximately four o'clock this afternoon? Did you
then go out again, returning some time after half past four?"

"No, absolutely not. I did not come home at all until after
half past four, as I told you."

"Miss Winfield, we have a witness—Mrs. Hall, the owner
of this house—who states that at approximately four o'clock
this afternoon the sound of your piano was heard, that there
were voices raised in anger in your room, a thumping noise
was heard, and the quarrel abruptly ceased. We also have a
witness—Miss Leach, who resides upstairs—who saw you
leave the house through the side gate at approximately
twenty-five minutes past four and walk down the lane away
from Doughty Street. Can you offer any explanation for
this?"

Stunned, I shook my head. "There must be some mistake.
If someone was here, it certainly was not I."

"Were you expecting any visitors today?"

"No."

The Inspector showed me a crumpled sheet of paper, holding it carefully with a pair of tongs.

"This was found in the deceased's hand. Can you tell me
what it is?"

I saw that it was a photocopy of the first page of Marius

Hart's last nocturne. Suddenly tears filled my eyes. I remembered Max's interest in my project, our lovely trip to Wales, his charm and his affection for me. Could he really be dead? It seemed impossible.

I looked up at the Inspector, who I supposed read my emotion as an indication of guilt.

"It's a piece of music." I tried to swallow the sob rising to my throat.

"I can see that." His tone was dry. "What can you tell me about it?"

I told him briefly about my project and about finding the nocturne among the Hart papers in Wales. "It was Mr. Fordham who helped me to gain access to the materials. I simply cannot believe he's dead."

"Miss Winfield, were you on intimate terms with the deceased?"

I saw no point in concealing the truth. "Yes, occasionally."

"And had you quarreled with him for any reason?"

"No!"

The Inspector looked at me with a kind of fatherly pity in his eyes. "Miss Winfield, it would be better for you to tell the full truth now. Nothing can be gained by your denial."

"But I have told you the truth!"

"Then I am sorry but I shall have to ask you to come along with us to the police station. You may have a solicitor present, if you wish. Do you know someone you wish to call upon?"

A solicitor. My mind was blank. But of course—James! I had thought of him as a friend, not in his professional capacity.

"Yes, yes. Mr. James Hall. He lives in this house."

The Inspector's brows shot up. "Is he the husband of the lady in the next room?"

"No, her son."

"I see. You may certainly ascertain whether or not he wishes to represent you."

It did not occur to me then that the Inspector had every reason for wondering if the son of one of the chief witnesses against me would want to take my case. I asked the Inspector to leave a message for James, knowing that Mrs. Hall, whatever her reluctance, would not fail to tell her son what had occurred.

I was taken to the nearby Holborn Police Station in Theobalds Road. How often I had walked past its door, never dreaming that I could be detained there, least of all on a charge of murder. They took my fingerprints and placed me in a room with a tape recorder—a recent innovation, I was told by the young constable who remained with me.

Everyone was surprisingly courteous. I had eaten nothing since breakfast, and when they brought me a pot of tea and a plate of sandwiches, I ate mechanically and then realized that I felt much better for the food.

At last Inspector Kent came in and repeated his formal caution, explaining that my statement would be taped and could be used in evidence against me. Again he urged me to have a solicitor present, and again I insisted that there was no need as I was telling the full truth.

"I am sure Mr. Hall will be here soon," I said, "but meanwhile I have nothing to hide."

The Inspector then took me over the events of the day in great detail, probing and repeating his questions. I could do nothing but state again what I had already said. I could offer no theory to account for the voices heard in my room nor for Miss Leach's statement that she had seen me walk out of the gate before four thirty that afternoon. I reiterated that I had looked at my watch when I couldn't find my keys and that it was then twenty minutes before five. We checked my watch against the clock in the police station and it was accurate.

It was almost nine o'clock when I was told that my solicitor had arrived. The Inspector stepped out and after what seemed like ages to me the door opened at last and James came swiftly to the table, sat down in the chair across from me, and took my hand for one brief reassuring moment.

"I'm so sorry I couldn't come sooner. I went to dinner with a friend and got your message just now when I returned home. I have been talking with the inspector about the case."

I looked into his eyes and said simply, "I'm so glad you're here."

"Now, Jane, please tell me exactly what happened this afternoon."

I recounted again where I had gone and the horror of returning home to find Max's body on the floor of my room.

"Had you quarreled with Mr. Fordham?"

"No, not at all. We had had a disagreement last evening but not in any sense a quarrel. Then we went to dinner and parted on very good terms."

"I see. The police seem to believe that you engaged in a lovers' quarrel and that you struck him over the head."

"With what? I don't even know how Max was killed. I asked the inspector but he wouldn't tell me."

James looked at me gravely. "Apparently he was struck over the head with a heavy object. The weapon seems to be a bronze bust, which shows evidence of blood and tissue matching the wound. A preliminary check indicates that the only fingerprints found on the bust are yours. Can you tell me about that?"

For a moment my mind was utterly blank. Then I remembered.

"Of course. When I saw Max lying on the floor, I rushed around the end of the table and my foot struck something. I saw that it was my bust of Chopin, and I picked it up and pushed it out of the way so that I could kneel beside him."

"You were not still wearing your gloves?"

I thought for a moment. "No. I believe I had taken them off when I was searching through my handbag for my keys."

"Did you pick up the bust with both hands?"

"Yes, I'm sure I did. It's quite heavy, you know."

James looked thoughtful. "As I see it, the police regard the fingerprint evidence as very damaging. The inspector says he would be quite willing to consider the possibility that someone else had committed the murder before you returned, but with the evidence of my mother and Miss Leach, and only your fingerprints on the murder weapon, he has little alternative but to charge you with the murder."

There was a pause.

"James, you do believe that your mother heard music and voices in my room?"

"Yes, I do. What Miss Leach claims to have seen may be less reliable."

"It all seems so impossible, so unreal."

Once again James put his hand over mine for a moment. "Jane, it seems to me quite dreadful that not only should you lose someone who was very dear to you but that you should be falsely accused of his murder."

I looked at him gratefully. "You do believe me, don't you? But James, how can you be so sure that I didn't kill Max?"

"Oh, because I know you, Jane. You see, it's unlikely that you would bash anyone over the head, but any of us might be driven to anger under certain circumstances and do something rash. The point is that if you had done so, you would never lie about it. You would not run out of the house and return later, pretending to find the body. You would simply say, 'Look, I've done something dreadful. It was an accident, but I did it.'"

"Yes, you're right. That's exactly what I would do."

James stood up. "So you see, Jane, someone else *was* there, someone else *did* kill this man, and we must find out who it was!"

1 7

A fter James's reassuring declaration of his belief in my innocence, he strode to the door, saying, "I'll be back shortly. I must speak to Inspector Kent."

For the first time since the arrival of the police after I had found Max's body, I felt waves of relief flow over me. James knew that I was telling the truth. I could see why Inspector Kent would doubt my word, with all the evidence against me, but now there was someone who believed me.

Then James was back. "Here's what happens, Jane. I'm sorry to say that you will have to remain here for the night. Tomorrow we appear before the magistrate, where we shall enter a plea of Not Guilty. At that time we must ask that you be allowed to post a bail bond so that you need not be held in custody until your first hearing. We will need a fairly large sum of money. Is there someone who can help you?"

"Yes, my father, of course, but what can he do? It's Friday—the banks will be closed."

James looked at his watch and smiled. "Nine o'clock. It's only one o'clock in the afternoon in California, isn't it? Let's ring him at once."

I gave him several numbers to try, and in a few minutes he returned to report that he had reached my father in his office in Los Angeles.

"He was marvelous!" James grinned. "He said of course it was all nonsense that you would kill anyone and then try to conceal it. He's going straight to his bank and will take the first available flight to London. I've booked a room for him at the Edgar, at his request. It seems you have both stayed there before."

"Yes. It's near the British Museum." My eyes filled with tears, remembering former visits to London with my father.

"Good. Now, Jane, is there a responsible person here in London who can vouch for you?"

Ironically, my first thought was of Max—well-known, respected—and my heart lurched at the horror that was renewed each time I was recalled to the fact of his death.

Then I said to James, "Do you remember my friend Patch?"

"The young lady with the ginger hair? We met in the garden last summer, did we not?"

"Yes. Either she or her parents would help me, I know, but unfortunately they are abroad and I don't have an address for them."

"Is there anyone else?"

I shook my head. My life in London had been so full that I had made no effort to seek more friendships than those of

Patch, Max, and James himself. Suddenly I remembered one other possibility.

"Of course! Dr. Quentin may be back in London by now." I had told James one day how pleased I was that I had had the chance to talk over my project on Marius Hart with my professor, who was on a research leave from the university. "He has been in Scotland, I believe, working on an article he is preparing, but he expected to be back in London soon."

"Splendid! Where can we find him, do you know?"

"He was staying at a friend's flat. The number is in my book."

James went out and returned in a moment. "No answer, but I'll try again later on. If he is available, it will help to have another responsible person as well as your father to speak for you in court. I must go now. Try not to worry, and I'll see you tomorrow."

When James had gone the young constable returned and announced that Detective Chief Inspector Kent had gone off to attend the autopsy and that I would probably not be questioned any more that night.

"If you'll come along with me, miss—"

He led the way through a maze of corridors and finally unlocked the door to a cell. When I had entered and the door was locked behind me, I sat down weakly on a cot against the wall and stared in disbelief at the bars that blocked my freedom. This couldn't be happening. It was all a nightmare from which I would awaken. But if it was real, what then? Was this only the beginning of many years to be spent behind bars?

My heart beat rapidly, my breath came in short gasps. I felt a desperate need to break out, to know that I could walk through those bars, even if I had to come back in again, just to know that it was possible to be free. I could feel panic rising and an almost unbearable impulse to cry out, to beg someone to understand that it was all a mistake, that I didn't belong here.

Sternly, I told myself not to be a fool. This has happened to plenty of other people, both guilty and innocent. You're here and no one is going to take pity on you, so it's no use making a scene.

I took off my shoes and stretched out on the cot, pulling the blankets up to my chin. For hours I lay awake, going over and over the events of the day, clinging like a child to the two lifelines held out to me—my father was coming to help me, and James believed in me. At last I slept.

In the morning I was given tea and toast and taken in the company of a policewoman to the Clerkenwell Magistrate's Court, where after a long wait I was at last summoned to the courtroom. James pressed my hand quickly and said, "They're here!" and I saw my father and Dr. Quentin at the far side of the room.

Inspector Kent read the charge to the magistrate and a plea of Not Guilty was entered. Then began the argument for permitting me to be released on bail. Inspector Kent reported that the police had already obtained my passport from my room in Doughty Street and that he had no objection to bail so long as the passport was held. My father gave assurance of having the funds to post the bond and Dr. Quentin attested that he would be residing in London during the next month and would guarantee my reappearance in court. The magistrate declared that on a charge of such gravity as the present one, he was reluctant not to rule that the suspect be remanded in custody, but since Detective Chief Inspector Kent agreed to the request for bail, he would so rule.

The date of the hearing was set for the fourth of April, three weeks away. Various papers were signed, and I was at last permitted to go out to the waiting room, where my father took me in his arms.

"It's all right, dear," he murmured, "it's going to be all right." I only wished that somehow a miracle would happen to prove him right.

18

As we stood in the waiting room of the Magistrate's Court, my father and Dr. Quentin congratulated James on securing my freedom on bail.

James beamed. "It's actually Inspector Kent we must thank. The magistrate will usually go along with the detective in charge of the case, as he did here." Then James turned to me. "Jane, I must tell you that the police have sealed off your room until they have finished their investigations. Is there somewhere—?"

I stood bewildered. Somehow I had thought only of returning to the security of my cozy room. Now I realized that even if it were available, I could scarcely remain in the same house with Mrs. Hall and Miss Leach.

My father settled the matter. "We should be able to get you a room at the Edgar."

James said that he would ask the inspector for permission to bring me some of my things as soon as he could. "I must go now. Can I give anyone a lift?"

"I'd like to walk a bit," I said, looking at my father, who nodded assent. Dr. Quentin went off with James, promising to drop in at the Edgar later in the day.

My father rang up the Edgar and booked a room for me. Then we set off toward Gray's Inn Road. I noticed he was wearing cap, muffler, gloves, and overcoat. "Warm enough?" I asked.

He grinned. "These things looked preposterous when I left home, but fortunately I remembered winter in London."

"How did you get here so soon?"

"Simple. I called Gretchen and asked her to book me a flight. Went to the bank and withdrew the money from savings, had the bank give me a draft in pounds sterling, then dashed home and packed a bag. Gretchen took me to the airport for a three o'clock flight. Took a taxi from Heathrow this morning, dropped the bag at the Edgar, and here I am!"

"You haven't had any sleep?"

"Oh, yes, I dozed on the plane. Plenty of time to sleep later."

I looked at him affectionately. Short and stocky, his thinning hair streaked with gray, he walked briskly by my side, his buoyant spirit filling me with courage.

When we reached Gray's Inn Road my father asked, "How about some curry for lunch?"

"Sounds good!"

We found a taxi and went to a favorite Indian restaurant in the West End. When the first course came, I discovered to my surprise that I was ravenous. We ate in companionable silence for a time. Then my father leaned forward across the table. "When you are ready, dear, I want to hear exactly what happened."

I told him every detail of the day before, from the time I left the library until I opened my unlocked door and found Max's body lying on the floor.

Finally he said, "Jane, Gretchen and I have wondered about this for some time and now it is most important to know. Did you care deeply for this man? You have mentioned him in your letters many times, but we have had no clue as to your real feelings."

"He was a charming man—clever, witty, marvelous company. He was also vain, selfish, and egotistical. He was wonderful to me, but no—oddly enough, I was never truly in love with him."

"Thank heaven for that. It is still an appalling and dreadful thing, but it is a different kind of grief than you would suffer if that had been true."

"Yes."

"Now we come to a very important question. Do you know of anyone who had quarreled with Max or who had any reason to be angry with him?"

I had known this question would be coming. If James had not already asked me this, it was probably because he assumed the murder had been committed by someone unknown to me. Yet sooner or later he would ask me and I would have to answer. Now I looked at my father's face and saw his deep concern.

"Yes," I said reluctantly. "Max's son Alan has been extremely angry with him. The problem is that I cannot believe Alan could have done this. He is a gentle person. However desperate he may have been, I don't believe he would actually use violence."

Then I told my father the whole story of Alan's conflict

with Max, ending with the threats Alan had made only the night before the murder.

"I know it sounds very damning for Alan. But surely if he wanted to kill his father he would have ample opportunity without coming to my place to do it. And I would never believe that Alan planned it all out to implicate me. If he did kill Max, it must have been in a moment of anger."

My father looked thoughtful. "Of course, the first thing we must know is where Alan was at that time on Friday. If he can prove his presence elsewhere, he will be in the clear. We must tell James Hall about this immediately, and he can inform the police."

We talked on, going over and over the details of the case without coming to any useful conclusions. At last we took a taxi to the hotel, where my father went to his room to get some much-needed sleep. When I went into the room assigned to me, a few doors from his, I realized that I had absolutely nothing with me, not even a toothbrush. I was still wearing the clothes from the day before, and now I remembered that today was Saturday and the shops were already closed. In England everything stops at one o'clock on Saturday and doesn't come to life again until Monday morning.

Fortunately the desk clerk rang me an hour later to announce a visitor, and I went down to find James with my suitcase and a carryall filled with books and music.

"Inspector Kent was very decent about letting me bring your things. He believes they have done all they can in your room. It's still officially sealed, but he sent a constable along to see that nothing vital was disturbed as we packed these up. I rang up young Brenda to come and help me."

I remembered catching a glimpse of an attractive blond girl in James's office who was vaguely described as "doing her Articles," a procedure I took to be something like a graduate internship for solicitors.

"It was good of her to come out on a Saturday," I said.

James grinned cheerfully. "Oh, she's slave labor, poor dear. We all go through it, you know. I thought she would know what kinds of things you would need."

Leaving the bags to be sent up to my room, I led the way to a small lounge I remembered from previous visits to the hotel, where we sat down in a quiet corner.

"Dad is sleeping," I told James, "but he wants me to tell you about Max's son, Alan."

When I had finished the story of Alan's quarrel with Max and his threats on the night before the murder, James was electrified. "This is just what we need, Jane! Whatever you may think of Alan, here is someone with a real motive for killing Mr. Fordham. Does Alan know where you live?"

"Oh, yes, he dropped in one day to talk about his problems and ask me to help him out if I could."

James stood up. "Look here, I'll talk with Inspector Kent about this right away." Then he paused. "But first, I'm going to have a go at it myself. I'll be back in an hour or two."

When I went upstairs to unpack the bags, I found that Brenda had done an excellent job of selecting the things I would most need, including cosmetics and my blow dryer. I stepped gratefully into a steaming bath, washed my hair, and emerged feeling that the taint of a night in a prison cell had been at least momentarily washed away.

It was half past five when James returned and the small bar in the hotel was just opening. We ordered drinks and took them back to the little lounge where we had sat before.

James was frowning and looking as irritable as anyone with his usually sunny nature could manage. He plunged straight into his story.

"I decided to try to see Alan myself before speaking to Inspector Kent, so I went directly from here to the Fordhams'

house in Hampstead. A servant answered the bell and said
young Mr. Fordham was not at home, so I asked to see his
mother. She took my card, and to my surprise, Cynthia
Fordham herself appeared and brought me into a small sitting room.

"I said to her, 'You understand that I represent Miss Winfield?' and she sort of tossed her head and said, 'Yes, of
course. Poor girl. It would be far better for her to confess
straight away. I understand that she has been charged with
the murder. It's obvious that she and Maxwell quarreled and
she struck him in anger. You see, Max could be absolutely
infuriating, as no one knows better than I.'

"I ignored this and merely asked her if I might see her son
Alan. She said quickly, 'Oh, he's out at the moment, but I'm
sure he cannot help you. You see, he was here with me on
Friday afternoon. He came in shortly before four o'clock and
we had tea together.'

"I asked if someone could corroborate that and she said,
'No, I'm afraid not. Both Nora and Cook had been given the
afternoon free to go to a special event together. I made the
tea myself and we sat in the kitchen.' I said, 'And was your
son here when the police came to inform you of your husband's death?' She paused a moment too long and then said
carelessly, 'No, he had gone out shortly before they came.'

"Then I asked if I might speak with her daughter, Sheila,
and she said that was quite out of the question: Sheila had
been hysterical and was under the doctor's care. I noticed
that Cynthia herself, unlike her daughter, was scarcely prostrate with grief.

"Finally I asked, 'Why are you so certain Miss Winfield is
guilty?' and she frowned slightly. 'You see, Max has had
many affairs over the years and sometimes the poor little
things become quite desperate. A few months was as long as
most lasted. He was fond of variety, you see. The only one

who ever meant anything to him was Lady Muriel Crawford, as she then was. He was absolutely dotty about her after her first husband died. He would have divorced me then but in the end she wouldn't have him. That was when we agreed to pursue our separate lives. Yet recently, when I wanted to divorce, he refused and put up all sorts of obstacles. At any rate, little Miss Winfield will be all right. A jury will let her off, I'm sure, if she will throw herself on their mercy. You see, I *know* she had a motive—'

"At that moment a tall good-looking chap with graying hair walked into the room and stopped abruptly when he saw me. Cynthia said, 'Hugh, dear, this is Miss Winfield's solicitor.' He simply looked at me and said, quite pleasantly but firmly, 'Thank you for coming, sir, but we have nothing further to say.'"

James looked at me indignantly.

"Having tea with his mother, indeed! It's obvious Cynthia would lie through her teeth to save her precious son. I rang up Inspector Kent and told him the whole story. He was noncommittal, but I know he was extremely interested and will call them both in for questioning."

"But James, why was Max's wife so willing to talk to you? I'd have thought she would avoid you like the plague."

"I think she is afraid for her son and is anxious to develop a strong motive for you. By the way, it's awkward for me to ask you this, but was there any—er—cooling between you and Max?"

I smiled. "No, not at all. But even if there had been, I would not have been deeply disturbed. You see, I was never really in love with Max. Our relationship was rather—well, you might say—casual. We were seldom—that is, it was only occasionally that—"

I was annoyed to feel myself blushing. I'm getting as bad as

Patch, I thought. I looked up to see James beaming at me happily.

"How marvelous! I mean—that you were not in love with him! That is to say, it makes it easier for you in a way now, doesn't it?"

James seemed almost as flustered as I was, and we were saved from our awkwardness when we looked up and saw Dr. Quentin coming into the lounge.

"I thought I'd come along and see how you are, Jane, and if there's anything I can do to help. The flat where I'm staying is only a ten-minute walk from here."

"Thank you, Dr. Quentin, I'm fine." I hoped I sounded convincing.

"Please call me Andrew," he said to both of us. "In a time of crisis we can surely dispense with formalities."

James looked at me. "I'd like to tell Andrew about Alan Fordham, if I may?"

"Yes, of course." Suddenly I broke into a smile. "I just remembered something I had totally forgotten! Last year there was a rumor among the graduate students in the music department that Dr. Quentin—that is, Andrew—had helped the police to solve a murder case. Is it true?"

Andrew shook his head in a casual gesture of dismissal. "It's most flattering, but actually my contribution was not that significant. I certainly don't think of myself as a Sherlock Holmes."

I accepted his word at the time and thought no more about it, but in the end it proved to be Andrew who pointed the way to the final solution of the mystery that confronted us.

19

The next day—Sunday—my father and I spent a quiet day together. In the morning Gretchen phoned and talked with me.

"Jane, dear, I'm so sorry about all this. Arthur tells me you have been formally charged with the crime. There must be some terrible mistake."

I told her how grateful I was for her support.

In the afternoon my father and I went for a long walk along Oxford Street, looking idly into the shop windows. Anything was better than sitting in the hotel, we decided. Then we wandered along to Manchester Square and to the fine old house containing the Wallace Collection. The building had been handsomely refurbished since my father's last visit to London, and we both enjoyed seeing the paintings in their elegant new setting. There was something especially soothing to my lacerated spirit in the delicate fragility of the Fragonards and Nattiers of the French school and the elegance of those eighteenth-century ladies of Reynolds and Romney.

We had dinner at an Italian restaurant in Covent Garden and walked back to our hotel on its quiet street off Bloomsbury Square.

My father had booked his return flight for the next morning. "There is nothing I can do here, and with your solicitor and your professor to look after you, I know you're in good hands. Now, Jane, I have arranged for you to keep your room here at the Edgar and charge it to my credit card."

"Oh, Dad, you needn't do that. I can go back to St. Catherine's." The Edgar was an old-fashioned hotel and far from elegant, but it provided a private bath, a telephone, and a television in each room, none of which were available in the cheaper hotel where I had stayed when I arrived in London.

"No argument! You'll stay here at least until your court hearing in three weeks. Then we'll see." Unspoken but ominous was the thought in both our minds that if the result of the hearing was unfavorable, I might be held in prison until the time of the trial. We had already told James to inform his mother that I would be giving up the room in Doughty Street, and once the police released the room, I could go back there and pack up my belongings.

That night I lay in bed, unable to sleep, thinking again of what Cynthia Fordham had told James the day before. According to Cynthia it was Max's infatuation with Lady Muriel that had caused the initial rupture in their marriage, not Cynthia's infidelity, as I had supposed. Now Cynthia said that she had wanted a divorce for some time. Yet when we were in Wales, Max had told me that he was willing to part but his wife was not. Which was the true story? And why would either of them lie about it? What did Cynthia mean by saying that she *knew* I had a motive?

Then there was the puzzle of Lady Muriel. If she had eventually refused Max in the past, as Cynthia declared, why was she asking him to meet her for lunch at the Savoy? Was she growing bored with Dods and perhaps regretting her decision?

Earlier that evening, my father and I had gone over and over these and a hundred other questions with James and Andrew, and none of us had come up with the answers to any of them. Andrew had been with me at the Savoy when Max and Lady Muriel came through the lounge and were seen by Lord Dodson. Everyone agreed that Dods must have learned somehow that his wife would be there, and I told them how painful it must have been for him to engage in such spying.

Only one helpful item came out of all our discussion, and that was a theory to account for how Max gained entrance to my room on the day he was killed. Andrew asked if Max might have picked up my keys by mistake, and in a flash the likely answer came to me. On the evening before the murder, when we returned from our dinner date, Max had taken my keys to open the door of my room because I was carrying some books he had brought for me. Usually I opened the door myself but I remembered his saying, "Give me either the keys or the books" and I handed him the keys. When he opened the door, I went straight to the table to unload the books. Since I didn't see the keys again, he must have absentmindedly dropped them into his pocket and come back the next afternoon to return them. When he didn't find me at home he simply let himself in to wait for me. Of course! Why hadn't I thought of that before?

James was delighted. "This shows you need not have been

there earlier to let Max in, as the police believe. We may not be able to prove it, but at least we can offer a reasonable explanation for Max's being there *before* you came home."

James had arranged that on Monday afternoon, after my father's departure, we would retrace where I had gone on the afternoon of the murder in the hope that someone might remember having seen me.

During the night there had been a light fall of snow, which was already melting, leaving an icy slush on the pavements. When he called for me, we set off for the starting point at the University of London Library.

James checked his watch. "It's almost half past three now. You believe this was about the time you left here on Friday?"

"Yes, as nearly as I can remember."

"All right. Now to Charlotte Street. Were you strolling or walking briskly?"

"Oh, briskly, I'm sure. It's too cold to stroll!"

"All right. We may be a bit slower today because of the ice, but we can allow for that."

In ten minutes or so we arrived at Patch's door beside the delicatessen, where the Gorgon had told me that Patch had left in a taxi sometime earlier.

"Now where?"

I led the way into Tottenham Court Road.

"Let's see. I went in here, looked at the blouses on the rack, and wandered out again. No one could possibly have noticed me."

"Let's go in and ask anyway. No harm in that."

I agreed, but my prediction proved true. None of the saleswomen could remember having seen me. Although it was as I expected, I felt downcast.

"Cheer up," James said. "We'll find someone who'll remember you."

I forced a smile, inwardly thanking James for his confidence.

James smiled back. "Next?"

"I looked into the windows all along here, but I didn't go into any of the shops."

Then we came to the bar where I had stopped for coffee.

James swept into the long narrow room, where several people formed a queue at the self-service counter. Approaching the two middle-aged women employees, one behind the counter and the other at the cash register, James handed each one a card.

"Excuse me. May I ask if you were both here on Friday last at about this time in the afternoon?"

The woman behind the counter looked with interest at the card. "A solicitor, eh? What's the trouble, luv?"

"Were you both here on Friday afternoon?"

"Yes, we was here. What's up?"

"This young lady was here on Friday having a coffee at about this time. It would help us very much if you should remember having seen her."

Both women stared at me.

"I was reading a book," I said, "and I sat over there." I pointed to a table along the wall.

The woman at the cash register gestured us aside. "Excuse me." She reached past us to take money from the next customer in the line. Looking at me disdainfully she growled, "Does it look like we could remember anybody partickler here?"

I had to admit that it seemed unlikely. The woman behind the counter gave me a kindly smile but could only add, "She's right, y'know. If the Queen come in, we might take notice, but bar that—" She shrugged.

James thanked them and we took our leave.

"I knew it was hopeless, James. It's not the kind of place where anyone would be remembered."

"Still, it was worth a try. One of them might have said, 'I remember the young lady because she's the spittin' image of my niece in Norfolk—always has her nose stuck in a book, she has, and I says to meself, she looks for all the world like Marlene!'"

I giggled at James's rendition of the Cockney. "I only wish there had been a Marlene!"

James grinned. "So do I. Now, about how long were you in the coffee bar?"

"Oh, only a short while. It was too crowded to linger for long."

"Then that brings us to close on four o'clock. Now where?"

"This way." We crossed the road and went along Great Russell Street to the bookshop where I had stopped to browse. James gave his card to the young man at the desk, whose stringy blond hair and pale eyes I vaguely remembered.

At James's question he looked at me and shrugged. "I don't know. I may have seen her before. Couldn't say when."

"I've been here with my friend, Patch Crawford. Do you remember a rather tall girl with red hair who plays the cello?"

"I might if I saw her. Don't know anyone's name, of course."

James turned to me. "Where were you standing most of the time?"

"Back here." I led the way to the fiction shelves at the back of the shop, well out of sight of the young man at the desk. "You see, it's hopeless. If only Patch were here, it might jog his memory somehow. I am sure he is the one she was chatting with when we were here one day, so she must come in fairly often."

We gave it up and walked back into Great Russell Street and down Drury Lane, where we stopped for a coffee. I knew the same thought was in both our minds. At the very time that James's mother heard the angry voices in my room, I was in the bookshop. If we could only have found a reliable witness who saw me at that crucial time, it would have cleared me of suspicion.

James looked at his watch. "What time did you leave the bookshop?"

"I suppose it must have been about a quarter past four. It was absolutely pouring buckets and I couldn't find a taxi. I waited at the bus stop for a while and finally took the bus home. Needless to say, I saw no one who knew me or would remember me. By then it had stopped raining and was only misting. When I couldn't find my keys, I thought I would have to go to the front door. That was when I looked at my watch."

"Any reason why you looked at the time just then? The police may ask you that."

"They did and I told them."

"Well?"

I looked at James and smiled. "I was hoping you would open the door yourself and I wouldn't have to face your mother after what had happened the evening before."

Instead of returning my smile, James frowned. "You know, Jane, I've been thinking about that. You mentioned that you thought the person who followed you that evening looked vaguely familiar."

"I'm not at all sure. I may have imagined it."

"Yes, but suppose it was someone who knew you, or at least someone who was following you specifically, not just any woman walking along the street. Whoever it was may have come back to your room when Max was there, and he may be the person whose voice Mother heard. I have questioned her closely, and she is certain that one voice—the one raised in anger—was that of a man, but she cannot identify the other voice as that of either a man or a woman. Of course she assumed it was you because it was in your room, but she admits that the second voice was not clearly audible."

"Actually, when I first saw that someone was in my room I thought it might be the person who had followed me the night before. But when I saw it was Max, of course I forgot about that."

James walked with me to the corner near my hotel. "I must dash, Jane. I'll ring Andrew Quentin this evening. He wants to know how we fared this afternoon. I wish we had better news for him. He's truly concerned about you, Jane— as we all are."

When we had said good-bye and I went into the hotel, the desk clerk announced, "You have a visitor in the lounge, Miss Winfield."

Who could it be? I wondered. I had just seen James, and I knew Andrew was having a conference that day with someone concerning the article he was preparing.

As I entered the dimly lighted lounge, a figure arose from a chair. I heard a voice say, "Hi, Janie, how are ya?" and found myself face to face with Brian.

20

I stood immobilized in the middle of the room, staring at Brian. In all the horror of Max's death and my being charged with his murder, I had completely forgotten that Brian was coming to London at about this time.

"When did you get here?" My voice sounded hoarse and unreal to my ears.

Brian tried his best smile of boyish charm. "Oh—er—I got in yesterday and slept most of the day. Jet lag, you know."

I simply stared at him and said nothing.

"Say, Janie, can't we sit down?" He took a few steps toward a sofa behind him. When I didn't move, he came back and reached out toward me.

"Come on!"

As his hand touched my elbow I flinched back instinctively. Then I moved slowly to a chair and Brian sat on the
sofa at my right.

He leaned toward me, a lock of fair hair falling over his
forehead. "It's been a long time. You're looking great! Look,
Janie, I know I was rotten to you and I'm really sorry. I can
make it up to you, I promise." His face wore the expression
of the naughty boy who knows he will be forgiven, a look I
remembered well.

Still I said nothing and Brian went on.

"Look, I heard some really bad news about you. I went
over to your place on Doughty Street this morning and your
landlady, Mrs. Hall, says you were arrested for killing some
man you had been seeing."

"Yes, that's right."

"I asked her what happened and she says you had a fight
with this guy, hit him over the head, and ran out, and then
you came back in as if you had just found him. Is that right?"

I felt a surge of renewed anger at Mrs. Hall. How could
she say all this to Brian, a perfect stranger? "No, Brian, it's
only what she *thinks* happened. It isn't true. I simply came
home and found him on the floor of my room. He was already dead."

"So who was he, anyway? If you came home and he was
already in your room—?"

I looked straight into his eyes. "Yes, Brian, we were lovers,
if that's what you mean. But I didn't kill him."

A look passed over Brian's face that could only be described as crafty. "Yeah, sure, I see. I'll tell you what, Janie.
I don't think you have anything to worry about. You get a
good lawyer and a good jury and they'll let you off like a
shot."

I stared at Brian in disbelief. I had lived with this man for
more than two years and spent another two years of my life

grieving over him. And suddenly I realized that he didn't know me at all. James Hall, with only our sporadic friendship to guide him, had understood me unerringly.

I felt like Titania when the pixie dust had worn off. The magic was gone. There he sat—undoubtedly handsome, with the same gray-green eyes and thick fair hair that had always filled me with enchantment—and now he seemed like a quite ordinary and thoroughly unlikable character. Could this really be the person I had cared for with such intensity?

I saw no point in trying to convince Brian of my innocence. I merely said, "I do have a good solicitor and he will be briefing a barrister to represent me in court. I know they will do their best for me."

Brian looked slightly belligerent. "The landlady told me it's her son who's your lawyer. I guess you know him pretty well?"

I could see that out of sheer habit Brian was building up to jealous anger.

Wearily I replied, "No, he's just a friend."

Brian looked sulky and unconvinced. We talked a few minutes longer. He told me where he was staying in London and that he would be going to Bristol and Bath from time to time to pursue his research.

Finally he said, "Well, I suppose I ought to be going now. I'll keep in touch. You take care, Janie. You know you'll always be my girl."

When Brian had gone, I began to feel a marvelous sense of relief creeping over me. At last I was beginning to be free of the obsession that had haunted my life for so long. Why this hadn't happened before I would never know, but it was enough that the spell was broken now. I knew it would never return. A good thing Brian had not arrived in London earlier than yesterday, I thought. I could imagine his senseless fury if he had come to my room and found Max there. I knew that for Brian, once he had decided that I belonged to him again, his own past actions ceased to exist and he would be as possessive as if we had never parted. It would never occur to him that I wouldn't come back gladly when he called.

The next afternoon James came again, bringing me my mail from Doughty Street. I told him about my visit from Brian the afternoon before.

"Is this the chap whose letter distressed you?"

I smiled, remembering James's kindness to me that day in his office.

"Yes, but it's all right now. Once I saw him again, I realized the feeling is gone, dissipated into thin air. I seem to have come to my senses at last."

For one brief moment, James put his hand over mine. "I'm so glad. Look, Jane, would you rather he didn't come to see you again? Where is he stopping? I can tell him to stay away, if you like."

"Yes, I'd be grateful if you would. He's at the Larchmont Hotel in Bedford Place."

"Then I'll pop round and see him one day soon. Actually, I have some news for you, but it's not at all helpful. I finally tracked down young Alan and he sticks like glue to the story that he was having tea with his mother at the time of the murder. He says Inspector Kent has questioned both of them—Alan and his mother—and is satisfied with their statements, so he doesn't see the need for being questioned by me. But, Jane, I'm convinced that Alan is lying. He seems to me to be a chap who is normally truthful and is now making rather a bad job of deceit. What I don't see is how he can stand by and let you be accused if he really is the guilty party."

"Perhaps he's sure I will get off and is planning to come

forward if I don't. It doesn't seem in character, but I may have been quite wrong about him."

"Also, I have been on to the Fordhams' solicitor. Apparently all three—the wife, the son, and the daughter—will benefit. As Max told you, the children's trusts terminate with Max's death, and I learned that the wife is still his principal beneficiary, so there must be a whopping sum for all of them."

I looked at him with concern. "James, you are spending so much time on all of this. Can you manage with your other clients?"

"Oh, well, we are dumping rather a lot of extra work on Brenda. I've promised her a bang-up dinner as a reward."

"I'm terribly grateful."

The clear blue eyes looked at me gravely. "Your case *is* rather important, you know. Now, no more nonsense. I must dash!"

After James had gone I went upstairs to my room and when I opened the packet of mail he had brought, I found the current copy of *Apollo.* I felt a stab of pain. It still seemed impossible that Max was dead. Automatically I looked for his column and there it was—the last he would ever write, I thought. It opened with warm words of praise for a contemporary work I regarded as particularly unattractive. How odd that he was so enthusiastic. Then I looked at the date of the concert. Wednesday, March 12. But he wasn't in London on that date. Of course, this was the concert he had asked me to cover for him and I had refused because I would be in Birmingham. Someone on the staff must have done it for him after all.

I laid the magazine aside and sat staring into space. If only Patch were here. I desperately needed the comfort of her crooked smile and her reassuring presence. Besides, there was a real possibility that if she walked into the bookstore with me, the young man could see us together and it might jog his memory about my being there on the day of the murder. But it was already four days ago. With each day that passed, it was less likely that he would recall anything from that Friday. By the time Patch returned from her concert tour it would be far too late to help.

On Friday, just one week after the day of the murder, James took me to the chambers of the barrister he was briefing to represent me in court. According to British custom, the client never sees the barrister except in the presence of the client's solicitor, and I was happy to have James with me.

Sir Albert Caldwell, Q.C., was a tall thin man wearing wire-rim glasses and a general air of disdain.

"I believe Mr. Hall has explained to you the nature of the hearing scheduled in two weeks' time?"

"Yes."

Sir Albert explained it to me anyway. "This is called a preliminary or committal hearing, held in Magistrate's Court, to determine whether or not you should be held for trial. If you are so committed, the trial will be scheduled at the Old Bailey. With the crowded state of the court calendar, it will probably be several months before the trial takes place."

"I see."

"At Magistrate's Court we have asked for what is known as an 'old-style' hearing, in which the Prosecutor for the Crown will call witnesses but in which we do not present a case for the defense. Nor do you yourself appear on the witness stand at this time. Our advantage is that we may cross-examine the witnesses and that we shall have before us the case for the Crown."

"I understand."

Sir Albert took off the wire-rim glasses and put them on

again. "Now, Miss Winfield, will you please tell me in your own words what occurred on the day of the crime?"

I recounted as clearly as I could the events of that Friday.

"You are aware of the evidence of Mrs. Hall, I believe? Can you account for her hearing the music of the piano in your room if you were not yourself present?"

"Yes, of course. If Mr. Fordham had come to return my keys, as I suppose, and let himself in to wait for me, it is very likely that he would go to the piano and play some of the music there. He was a first-rate amateur pianist, and he had taken a particular interest in the project on which I am working."

"I see. Now, can you account for the voices heard by Mrs. Hall and the evidence of the lodger—Miss Leach—that you were seen going out of your room before half past four on that day?"

"No, I can't. I know that Miss Leach rather dislikes me—"

"A repressed spinster of the classic variety," James put in.

I nodded. "And I'm afraid Mrs. Hall disapproves of me too." I glanced apologetically at James. "But I would not expect their hostility to extend to inventing evidence against me."

Sir Albert adjusted his glasses again. "Miss Winfield, despite the assurances of your solicitor that you are innocent of this crime, it is my duty to urge you now to tell the full truth if you have not done so already. You must understand that if you struck a blow in anger, unaware of its possibly fatal consequences, and then returned to find Mr. Fordham dead, we would have a much stronger case for clemency on the part of the jury than if you attempt to conceal your action."

"Yes, I do see that but I simply can't confess to something I didn't do."

Sir Albert very nearly shrugged. "One further question. I have spoken with Mr. Hall about the awkwardness of his mother's being a witness against you in this matter. I must ask you now if you still wish to retain Mr. Hall as your solicitor."

I looked at Sir Albert in alarm. "Oh, yes, I do want Mr. Hall, very much. It's all right, isn't it?"

"Yes, certainly, if you have no objection."

I smiled with relief, and after some further discussion between James and Sir Albert about details pertaining to the hearing, we took our leave.

Standing outside, where a pale, watery sun had broken through the clouds, James said, "I'm so sorry I must run. Will you be all right?"

I must have looked as bleak as I felt. "How can Sir Albert help me? He doesn't believe me, does he?"

"Well, I'm afraid not. But that isn't necessary for him to defend you. Oddly enough, although he doesn't look the type, he has had considerable success in criminal trials. That's why I wanted him. He is persistent, and he takes a personal pride in his cases."

"But he seemed so hostile to me."

"No, he wants to form an estimate of how you would fare under cross-examination if we go to trial. But that is looking a long way off. We must somehow find a solution to this puzzle, Jane, before it comes to that."

21

About nine o'clock that same evening James came to my hotel, and we sat in our usual chairs in the corner of the lounge.

"I hope you don't mind my calling at this hour."

"Of course not."

"I want to let you know about my visit to your erstwhile friend Brian."

I had told James how Brian had left me twice for another girl, and I knew that he was prepared to dislike Brian on sight.

"I went to his hotel about half an hour ago and found him in. He asked me up to his room and handed me a drink. 'It's good bourbon,' he told me. 'I got it at the Duty Free.'

"I took the glass and sat in the only chair while he perched on the bed. I told him that as your solicitor I had come to say that you preferred not to have visitors before your committal hearing, which is scheduled for the fourth of April. He looked at me with a sort of grin and said, 'I suppose you mean she doesn't want to see *me*. She was pretty cool when I saw her the other day. I don't really blame her. She has good reason to be mad at me, but she'll get over it.'

"At that moment a buzzer sounded on the wall by the door. Brian said, 'Excuse me, that must be a phone call for me. I'll be right back.' When he had gone out to take the call at the telephone in the passage, I noticed his passport lying on the table at my elbow. Idly, I picked it up and flipped the pages. You can imagine my surprise when I saw the entry stamp was dated *13 March, Heathrow*. That was Thursday of last week, and he told you he hadn't arrived in London until Sunday.

"When he returned I asked him about this. At first he flared up and said, 'What do you mean, messing about in my things?'

"With some effort, I kept my temper and merely repeated my question. He seemed to be thinking about what answer to make. At last he said that there was an explanation but he didn't see why he should tell *me* about it. He said, 'Tell Jane I'll explain it to her myself. I'll be over to see her tomorrow afternoon about three.'"

I sighed. Brian would not be easily discouraged, I knew.

"I think I may as well see him tomorrow. We'll find out why he lied, and maybe I can convince him that I truly don't want to see him again."

I thanked James once more for his efforts, and we talked on for a little while before he took his leave.

Brian arrived the next afternoon, wearing a sheepish grin but looking supremely confident. I could see that it never occurred to him that I might really have ceased to care for him. He was sure that I was merely piqued and he could easily regain my affection.

"Hi, Janie. Did you really tell that lawyer you didn't want to see me?"

"Yes."

"Look, I'm sorry about everything but it's going to be OK from now on." He put on a serious expression. "It's been miserable for me too."

I failed to see the logic of this, and since his feigned repentance left me quite unmoved, I simply changed the subject.

"Why did you tell me you didn't arrive in London until Sunday?"

"Oh, that. Well, to tell you the truth, I did come in on Thursday morning of last week. I slept all afternoon and then decided to go and see where you lived. I showed them your address at my hotel and they told me to walk around the corner of Russell Square and follow Guilford Street until I came to your street. Just as I passed the subway station I saw you come out and decided to follow you. I didn't want to speak to you yet because you had written that you didn't want to see me. So I thought I would just go along and check things out first. You understand what I mean?"

"No, I can't say that I do."

"Well, you might be living with some guy, for all I knew. Anyway, it was really foggy and getting thicker every minute. I guess I scared you because you finally ran up to the door and started yelling for help. Well, of course I didn't want to admit that I had followed you so I just told you I came in on Sunday. I didn't know some nosy lawyer would be snooping around looking at my passport."

I let this pass. "Then why did you wait until Monday to look me up again?"

"Well—er—I went out of town for the weekend to check

out some things for my project. I came back Sunday evening and went over to your place the next morning."

"What time did you leave London on Friday?"

Brian's eyes narrowed. "Wait a minute! 'Where was I at the time of the murder?' Is that what you mean?"

"It's not an unreasonable question."

"Well, at four o'clock I was on the train to Bristol."

The time of the murder had been in the newspapers, I knew.

"Where did you stay in Bristol?"

"At the Hotel Commodore. I checked in some time in the evening."

"What time?"

Brian looked at me resentfully. "What is this, the third degree?"

"Why not?"

"Well, I don't remember what time it was. I ate dinner somewhere near the station and then went on to the hotel." Suddenly Brian looked at me suspiciously. "Say, that lawyer fellow who came to see me lives in the house in Doughty Street, doesn't he? He must be the guy that gave you the big reception that night in the fog and then closed the door. I suppose he's more than just your lawyer, huh? That was quite a clinch."

I felt nothing but disgust at this. When Brian then proceeded to declare his undying love for me I was pleased to note that I felt no stir of response. At last I told him good-bye and asked him firmly not to come back until after my court hearing. I thought it best to set a specific time limit that he might be willing to observe.

"OK, if that's what you want. I'll be in and out of town anyway. So, take care, Janie. I'm sure they'll let you off!"

When Brian had gone I thought how ironic it was that he was the man who had followed me in the fog that night and

caused such terror. The killer of the women had been arrested just two days earlier, and I was glad to know that I had
not been a potential victim. But how like Brian to do something stupid and then lie about it, whether it was murder or
merely an embarrassing act.

The next day James told me that my room at Doughty
Street was now unsealed.

"If you'll pop your things into boxes," he said, "I'll come
round into the lane with the car at about half past five and we
can take them to your hotel."

Since the police still had my keys, I had to ring the bell to
be admitted by Mrs. Hall when I went to the house at about
four o'clock. She greeted me coldly and stepped aside so that
I could come in.

"I have unlocked the door to your room, Miss Winfield.
My son informs me that he will assist you in taking away
your things."

I took a deep breath and tried to keep my voice steady.
"Mrs. Hall, please. I want you to know that I was not in my
room that day when you heard the piano and the voices. I
don't know who it was, but it was someone else—"

She simply gave me a freezing look. "You will have to
excuse me. It is not appropriate for us to discuss this matter
outside of the courtroom." And she marched into her sitting
room and closed the door. Of course, I thought bitterly, it
was four o'clock. No doubt her tea was getting cold.

I was so angry that when I went into my room, where I
had lived contentedly for nine months, the heat of my resentment carried me past the first wave of nostalgia I would otherwise have felt.

"She might at least be willing to listen," I muttered, stuffing the items from my kitchen shelf into one of the cartons

James had left for me. "Her own son believes me. Why can't she?"

As I went on packing my suitcases and filling the cartons with assorted items, I realized that my bronze bust of Chopin was missing. Of course, Exhibit A—the murder weapon. My mind started around its familiar track. If someone else had used the bust to strike Max, why were only my fingerprints on it? Either the person was wearing gloves or it had been wiped clean before I picked it up from the floor on that fatal day.

When I had nearly finished my packing, I made myself a cup of tea and sat down with my feet up on a carton, sipping the fragrant brew. I had left the inner door open, expecting that James would be along shortly, when I looked up and saw Miss Leach standing in the passage staring at me in surprise.

I was equally startled and found myself saying, "Won't you come in?" before I remembered the awkwardness of the circumstances.

"Oh!" she said, putting one hand to her cheek. "Thank you, but—that is, I don't know—"

I looked at the timid woman in front of me and felt almost sorry for her. "Look, Miss Leach, you needn't be afraid. I haven't murdered anyone, whatever you may think."

She pressed her lips together primly. "Oh, Miss Winfield, I didn't say—I mean, I could only tell what I saw, couldn't I? I'm sure I would never wish to accuse anyone falsely."

I put down my cup and walked toward her. She took a step backward as if she half expected me to attack her.

I spoke softly, looking directly into her eyes. "Miss Leach, can you be sure of the time you believe you saw me on that day? Could it possibly have been later than the time you told the police?"

Now her hand went to her mouth and she backed away, shaking her head from side to side. "No, no! It was exactly what I said it was! You must excuse me now—" And she fled up the stairs.

As I turned back toward my room, the front door opened and I saw Mr. Emery coming slowly down the passage. He saw me and came straight toward me, a look of compassion on his kindly face. Putting his hand gently on my arm, he murmured, "My dear young lady. My dear young lady."

"Hello, Mr. Emery," I said, feeling the sting of tears behind my eyes.

He looked at me gravely. "You didn't do this thing, did you?"

"No, I didn't."

He nodded his head up and down. "No, I thought not. James Hall says you are innocent, and I believe him. A fine young man. Yes, yes. A fine young man. The truth will come out, my dear. Never fear, the truth will come out." And with another pat on my arm, he took himself slowly off toward the stairs.

In a few minutes James came along and we loaded all my belongings into his car and set off for the Edgar. I told him about my attempts to speak to his mother and to Miss Leach, and he merely shook his head.

"I know, Jane. Needless to say, I have tried but to no avail."

Then I told him about Mr. Emery's kindness. "He's a darling!" I exclaimed.

"And he's a wise old gentleman. I wish there were more like him."

In the two weeks remaining before my hearing I lived in a state of dazed unreality. As day after day passed it was clear that the case had reached a dead end. All hopes of finding a witness who had seen me at the time of the murder had faded. No new evidence appeared to shed any light on the mystery of Max's death.

I found myself withdrawing into a shell-like existence. In the mornings after breakfast I went for long walks, stopping for lunch somewhere, not because I was hungry but because it was something to do. Back in my room at the Edgar I spent the afternoons and evenings reading or watching television. Both James and Andrew several times invited me to dinner, but I shrank from going out or being around people. I kept snacks of cheese and fruit in my room, which I nibbled at for dinner, consuming pots of tea sent up by the hotel.

The pleasure of concerts and theaters that had formed such a vital part of my life in London seemed far away and unreal, and I found it utterly impossible to concentrate. I had put all the Marius Hart materials in the closet, apologizing to Andrew Quentin for being unable to go on with my work.

"It's hardly surprising," he had said reassuringly. "Don't worry about anything until this is all over."

One day when James had brought me my mail I found a postcard from Patch in Heidelberg. Although she wrote with British understatement I sensed that the tour was going well and that she was in seventh heaven. Dear Patch! I knew she would have no idea what had happened to me. She never read the news and would not have seen the item even if it had been carried in the local papers along her route, which seemed unlikely. She had left me no addresses because the group would be constantly on the move. Lady Muriel would have her itinerary, of course, but she and Dods were in Italy.

Patch's postcard ended, *Staying on in Frankfort for a week or so when tour is finished.* That would be long after my hearing on the fourth, I thought regretfully.

I tried not to think what might have happened by that date. If the charges were not dropped, would James and Sir

Albert be able to extend my freedom on the bond or would I be committed to prison to await my trial?

Shortly before the day of the hearing the newspapers began running the story of the murder again, with a new element added. At first there had been straightforward accounts of the death of the distinguished music critic, son of the renowned conductor. Now some enterprising journalist had learned about the music Mrs. Hall had heard and about the score found in Max's hand and had dubbed the case "The Nocturne Murder." Apparently the item was picked up by a news service, for my father found the same phrase used in the Los Angeles *Times*.

On the evening before the hearing, James came for a last interview. "Since we don't have to present a case for the defense," he said, "you won't be called upon to testify. What Sir Albert wants to do is to probe for any weaknesses in the case for the Crown. In his cross-examination he hopes to turn up facts we may not be aware of."

When James had gone I knew that he had done his best to be consoling, but I also knew that he had no real hope that at the hearing the next day the charges against me would be dropped.

22

The committal hearing took place in the same room in the Magistrate's Court in which I had been formally charged with Max's murder three weeks before. Again I sat on a bench on a raised platform with a railing in front. James sat a few feet in front of me, facing the magistrate and with his back to me. James explained that if I wished to speak to him during the hearing I might ask the attendant to secure his attention. Sir Albert sat at a separate desk at a right angle to James and to his right. At the left, and facing Sir Albert across the Court, was the barrister who was leading for the Prosecution, a young Asian who looked to be about my age.

"We have young Chatterjee," James had murmured to me

as we came into court. "His family are from Calcutta, I understand. He's first-rate."

I wasn't sure that having a first-rate barrister against us was necessarily good but I understood that James was expressing a professional opinion of the young man's competence.

When the magistrate entered everyone rose. I remembered him as having presided the day I was charged, a distinguished man in his fifties, with thick wavy hair going gray at the temples.

The formalities began with a repetition of the charge and of the plea of Not Guilty. Then the first witness—Mrs. Myrtle Hall—was called and took the oath.

Mr. Chatterjee began the questioning.

Q: "Mrs. Hall, will you please tell us what occurred at your home on the afternoon of Friday the fourteenth day of March of this year?"

A: "Yes. I was upstairs in my bedroom when I heard someone calling out below. It proved to be Miss Winfield, my ground-floor lodger. She said there had been an accident and was preparing to ring for an ambulance. I looked through the open door into her room and saw a man lying on the floor. When I examined him I saw that he was dead."

Q: "How could you be certain that he was dead and not merely unconscious?"

A: "I was in nursing service in the war for five years, part of that time in military hospitals. I have seen many men dead and dying."

Q: "Did you see any wound on the body?"

A: "Yes. There was a severe contusion above the left temple and a small amount of blood where the skin had broken."

Q: "Did you recognize the man?"

A: "Yes. His name was Maxwell Fordham. He had visited Miss Winfield regularly for some months."

Q: "What did you do next?"

A: "I rang for the police."

Q: "At about what time was this?"

A: "At about a quarter to five, I should think."

Q: "Now, Mrs. Hall, can you tell us please what took place within the hour before your examination of the body?"

A: "Yes. I was in the kitchen, opposite Miss Winfield's room, where I heard the sound of the piano. Then the music stopped and I heard voices in the room."

Q: "At about what time was this?"

A: "It was shortly before four o'clock when I heard the music."

Q: "And then?"

A: "The music stopped and the voices began. They sounded angry, as if an argument or quarrel was in progress."

Q: "How can you be sure of the time?"

A: "I always have my tea at four o'clock. As I carried my tray from the kitchen down the passage to my sitting room, I heard the voices."

Q: "Were both voices raised in anger?"

A: "The man's voice certainly was. The other voice was not as audible."

Q: "Then you cannot state absolutely that the second voice was that of Miss Winfield?"

A: "Not precisely. However, Miss Winfield rarely had other visitors. Who else could it be?"

Sir Albert (rising): "Objection!"

Magistrate: "Sustained." (To Mrs. Hall): "Please answer the question without elaboration."

Q: "Did you hear anything further?"

A: "Yes. A few moments later, I had entered my sitting room and was adjusting the dial on the telly when I heard a sort of thud."

Q: "Would you describe this as the sound of a person falling to the floor?"

A: "No, it was more like the sound of a heavy object falling."

Q: "And after that?"

A: "Then I closed the door to the sitting room and watched my program on the telly. I could hear nothing further."

Q: "At what time did you go upstairs?"

A: "At half past four, when the program ended."

Q: "You took your tray back to the kitchen first?"

A: "Yes, of course. I placed the cup and plate in the dishwasher and went up to my bedroom."

Q: "And you heard nothing at this time?"

A: "Nothing."

Q: "That will be all."

Sir Albert rose with regal dignity to cross-examine.

Q: "Mrs. Hall, you have said that it was at approximately four o'clock that you heard the voices in Miss Winfield's room. Although you normally have your tea at about that time, is it possible that on this particular day it might have been a few minutes earlier or a few minutes later than that time?"

A: "No. I looked at the clock in the kitchen and it was just on four o'clock when I scalded the pot."

Q: "So it was a few minutes after four as you came down the passage?"

A: "Yes. My program was just starting when I turned the dial. There are always some commercial messages before it properly begins."

Q: "Please remember that the charge in this case is murder. Any detail may prove to be of vital importance. Can you be absolutely certain of the time you have stated?"

A: "Yes, absolutely."

I could have told Sir Albert that he would make no head-

way with the Iron Lady. He evidently agreed, for he shifted
to another topic.

Q: "Now, Mrs. Hall, you have stated that Mr. Maxwell
Fordham had visited the defendant from time to time
over a period of several months. Had Miss Winfield introduced you to him or referred to him by name?"

A: "No."

Q: "Then can you explain how it was that you were able to
give Mr. Fordham's name to Detective Chief Inspector
Kent a short time after his arrival at the scene of the
crime?"

A: "Yes. I knew who he was."

Q: "Can you explain that, please?"

A: "Yes. He was the son of Sir Cyril Fordham, the conductor. I had seen Mr. Maxwell Fordham's picture in the
papers and I recognized him when he first called upon
Miss Winfield."

Mrs. Hall's tone was one of pure venom. It occurred to me
now that in addition to possessiveness over her son, she must
feel resentment at my acquaintance with someone she would
regard as an inhabitant of a glamorous world to which she
had no access.

When Mrs. Hall had stepped down, the doctor was called
who had come to examine Max's body. He testified that he
had examined the body at a quarter after five on Friday, the
fourteenth of March, and placed the time of death, according
to body signs, at approximately one hour earlier or less; that
is, between a quarter past four and half past four, but probably not earlier than four o'clock.

Next came the pathologist who had performed the post-
mortem.

Mr. Chatterjee: "Can you tell us please what was the
cause of the death of the deceased?"

A: "Yes. Death was caused by an epidural hematoma. That is to say, as a result of a blow to the head, an artery is torn on the surface of the brain, causing a blood clot which in turn results in death."

Q: "From the appearance of the wound, what kind of weapon or object could have caused the trauma?"

A: "There was no deep penetration of the head, as would occur in a knife wound, nor was there any mark indicating a weapon with a concentrated striking zone, such as a hammer. A best guess would be that the wound was caused by a blow being struck with a large rounded object of considerable weight."

Q: "Would such a blow require great strength to deliver?"

A: "Actually, no. The injury sustained would require a vigorous blow but not one of unusual strength. Furthermore, the blow appears to have been struck from above. That is, the victim may have been sitting or even kneeling, although this is conjectural. If the person striking the blow were standing above the deceased, the blow might have considerable force."

Sir Albert then arose to cross-examine.

Q: "Is death instantaneous in this kind of injury?"

A: "Not necessarily. After the blow is struck, the victim may move about, even speak, and subsequently lapse into a coma and die."

Q: "Then it is possible that a person might strike such a blow, leave the victim apparently alive and not seriously hurt, and be quite unaware of the fatal consequences of his act?"

A: "Yes. That is entirely possible."

I felt exasperated with Sir Albert for making such a point of this. I knew he did not believe my story and was trying to provide for extenuating circumstances in case I had struck Max and then come back to find him dead.

The next witness was Detective Chief Inspector Kent. He reported that the call to the police was placed at 4:47 P.M. and recounted his arrival at the scene of the crime and his procedures there. Then my bronze bust of Chopin was introduced into evidence.

Mr. Chatterjee: "Can you tell us, please, what was found on this exhibit?"

A: "Yes. On the back portion of the statue or bust were blood and tissue matching that of the deceased."

Q: "What conclusion do you draw from this?"

A: "That this was the weapon used to deliver the blow which proved fatal to the deceased."

Q: "Was the weapon tested for fingerprints?"

A: "Yes. There were full prints of both hands matching those of the defendant, Miss Jane Winfield. No other prints were found."

Q: "Thank you, Detective Chief Inspector."

Sir Albert rose. "We stipulate to this exhibit as the probable weapon used in the attack on the deceased. No questions."

I had already told James and Sir Albert that a few days before Max's death I had polished the bust with a soft cloth, so it was not surprising that the police had obtained a clear set of prints.

Miss Leach was now called as the next witness.

Q: "Will you please describe what occurred on the afternoon of the fourteenth of March?"

A: "Yes. At twenty-five minutes past four o'clock I looked out of my window and saw Miss Winfield open the gate opposite her outside door and step into the lane."

Q: "Will you please describe the arrangement of the house and how you were able to see what you did?"

A: "Yes. The house stands at the corner of Doughty Street and Wortle's Lane, with iron railings running along the front and side of the house. My bedroom is on the first floor at the front, with windows overlooking both the street and the lane."

Q: "How do you fix the time at which you saw Miss Winfield?"

A: "I had come home early from the office because I was suffering from a cold. I had finished my tea in front of the telly. The program I was watching ended at twenty-five minutes past four and a weather report began. It had been raining very heavily for a time and had then subsided. I stepped to the window above the lane to look out at the weather and then it was that I saw Miss Winfield going out of the gate."

Q: "In which direction did she go?"

A: "She turned to her right, away from Doughty Street, but there was a large lorry parked in the lane and I could not see where she proceeded from there."

Sir Albert began his cross-examination with an air of confidence.

Q: "Now, Miss Leach, your room is of course one story above ground level and therefore you are looking down upon any persons walking below. Were you able to see the face of the person you identify as Miss Winfield?"

A: "No, I could not see her face."

Sir Albert allowed a dramatic pause to fill the courtroom, even though there was no jury to impress at this preliminary hearing. He continued in a purring tone.

Q: "What was the person wearing?"

A: "A light-colored belted Burberry."

Q: "Is this not a garment similar to that worn by a good many young ladies in London at this time of year?"

A: "Yes, I suppose so."

Q: "And since you were looking down from above, can you state positively that it was Miss Winfield you saw and not another young lady of similar height in a light-colored belted burberry?"

A: "Yes, I can."

Q: "Will you explain that, please?"

A: (Scarcely concealing a triumphant little smile): "This young lady was wearing on her head a scarf with broad bands of color on the border and bright scarlet elephants in the center. Looking down, I could see these quite plainly on the top of her head. I have seen Miss Winfield wearing this scarf on a number of occasions. It appears to be a unique design."

Sir Albert continued to question Miss Leach about the time when she had seen "the person" going out of the gate but was unable to shake her insistence that it was precisely twenty-five minutes after four.

Finally Sir Albert sat down with regal dignity, concealing his dismay.

Suddenly I felt a rush of pure panic. I had known what sort of testimony Mrs. Hall and Miss Leach would give, but hearing it now in the full formality of the courtroom, given under oath, made it seem terrifyingly real and unanswerable. I remembered my one night in the cell at the Holborn Police Station and trembled at the thought of being convicted of this crime and sentenced to a long term in prison. With all the strength I could muster, I forced myself to push away the fear and keep my hold on sanity.

23

After Miss Leach's testimony, court was recessed for lunch. As I stepped into the waiting room I found my professor standing there.

"Andrew! I wasn't sure you were here."

He smiled reassuringly. "Yes, I was sitting directly behind you in what they call the visitors' gallery, although in a small courtroom like this one it isn't a gallery at all. It's just a little area with a long bench."

In a moment James joined us. "This neighborhood isn't the West End, I'm afraid. No terribly good restaurants nearby. But there's rather a decent pub in the next street if you'd care to go there."

The crowded and noisy pub proved to be just what I

needed. I clung to a small corner table while Andrew went to the bar for lagers and James queued up for plates of shepherd's pie. By the time they squeezed their way back to the corner and perched on tiny chairs, we were so engulfed in the crowd that serious conversation was impossible.

We talked a lot of nonsense about pubs we had known and loved and studiously avoided speaking of my case. It was obvious that there was nothing hopeful to say at this point. Mrs. Hall's evidence was all too convincing, and the only hope concerning Miss Leach was that she had unaccountably got the time wrong, a possibility which didn't offer much promise.

Back in Magistrate's Court, we settled into our places. The first witness to be called after the lunch break was Cynthia Fordham. Mr. Chatterjee began the questioning.

Q: "Mrs. Fordham, will you please describe the relationship between yourself and your late husband?"

A: "Yes. For some years we have lived independently. That is, we agreed to remain in the same household until the children were grown but with no marital ties."

Q: "Your children have now reached the ages of twenty-one and nineteen respectively, have they not?"

A: "Yes."

Q: "Then may I ask if you were still willing to continue with the—er—arrangement you have described?"

A: "I was not. For some time I have asked my husband to agree to a divorce and have met with opposition and finally with outright refusal."

Q: "Could you not institute proceedings yourself?"

A: "Yes, of course, but he would not agree to a reasonable financial arrangement."

Q: "I see. What reason did Mr. Fordham offer for his refusal?"

A: "He invoked his upbringing in the Roman Catholic Church. Although he had not entered a church for years, he insisted that he could not agree to be divorced. I believe the real reason was that he found marriage a convenience. Maxwell was frequently involved with women. Often these affairs were with young women who naively hoped that the affair would lead to marriage. Remaining married was a form of protection for him. He tired of each one rather quickly, I believe, and sometimes they became troublesome."

Q: "Now, Mrs. Fordham, were you aware of Mr. Fordham's—er—friendship with the defendant in this case?"

A: (disdainfully) "I knew Max had been seeing an American girl who lived in some dreary place like Bloomsbury. I did not know any further details about her until she killed him."

Sir Albert: "Objection!"

Magistrate: "Sustained." (To Cynthia, with heavy irony): "Mrs. Fordham, may I remind you that in the United Kingdom a defendant is presumed innocent until proven otherwise."

Cynthia (flippantly): "Sorry!"

Mr. Chatterjee: "Now, Mrs. Fordham, have you any evidence to present which might have a bearing on this case?"

A: "Yes. I have a letter from Paris addressed to my husband. The letter arrived on the day after his death. Naturally I opened it."

The letter was placed in evidence and the magistrate asked the clerk to read it.

Clerk (in a matter-of-fact voice): "'Max, *mon trésor*—'"

Magistrate (with raised brows): "'*Mon trésor*'?"

Mr. Chatterjee: "A term of endearment, I believe, sir."

Magistrate: "Hmph."

Clerk: "'I am trying my English in this letter to you. I am
so happy since you come to Paris to see me. Two weeks
only until I come to London and again you hold me in
your arms. I adore you, my *darling*. How you laugh
when I say "darling" in English! I love you, I adore you.'
Signed, 'Marie.'"

Q: "Now, Mrs. Fordham, will you explain the relevance of
this letter to the present hearing?"

A: "Of course. My husband had made several trips to Paris
in recent weeks to look after affairs connected with his
mother's estate. Clearly he had formed a new liaison
there and, following his usual pattern, was no doubt cooling toward"—for the first time, Cynthia looked directly at
me—"this young lady."

When Sir Albert arose to cross-examine, I knew that after
Miss Leach's evidence of the scarf he must have had little heart
for the case, but he dutifully attempted to do what he could.

Q: "Has the girl Marie come to London to your knowledge,
Mrs. Fordham?"

A: "No. I wrote telling her of Max's death and have heard
nothing further."

Q: "Mrs. Fordham, may I suggest to you that merely because
some ladies became strongly attached to the late Mr.
Fordham and became 'troublesome,' as you put it, when
he attempted to terminate their relationship, it does not
follow that this was true of Miss Winfield."

A: "No, I suppose not."

Q: "If, in fact, Miss Winfield was not, shall we say, deeply
attached to the late Mr. Fordham but merely enjoyed his
company from time to time, then the letter you have presented would have little significance, is that not so?"

A: "If that were true, of course."

Cynthia's tone implied that such a hypothesis was unlikely.

Sir Albert subsided with an air of having made the best of a bad job. It was obvious that no one would believe that I was impervious to the charms of the devastating Max.

Now Alan Fordham came to the witness box.

Mr. Chatterjee: "Mr. Fordham, you are aware, I believe, of a letter written to your father by a young woman in Paris and received after his death?"

A: "Yes. My mother showed me the letter."

Q: "Did the deceased—your father—make any statements to you regarding the person who wrote this letter?"

A: "Yes, he did. On the morning of the day of his death, he told me that he was seeing a beautiful girl in Paris."

Q: "Did your father usually confide in you concerning his—er—friendships with women?"

A: "Not exactly, but I was sometimes aware of them."

Q: "Then can you explain why he did so on this occasion?"

A: "Yes. He told me that Marie—that was the girl's name—had a friend who was nineteen." A slow flush began to appear across Alan's face. "He said that Marie and her friend were coming to visit in London and he wanted me to become acquainted with Marie's friend, who wished to meet a young English gentleman."

Q: "Were you aware at this time of Mr. Fordham's relationship with the defendant at this hearing?"

A: "Yes, I was."

Q: "Are you in fact personally acquainted with her?"

A: "Yes. We have met several times."

Q: "Did you question your father concerning Miss Winfield?"

A: "Yes. When he told me about Marie, I said, 'What about Jane?' And he sort of shrugged and made a flip reply."

Q: "Can you be more specific, please?"

A: "He said something like, 'Jane doesn't know about Marie, and I shall take care that she doesn't find out.'"

Q: "Thank you, Mr. Fordham."

Sir Albert rose with impressive dignity.

Q: "Mr. Fordham, is it not true that you had quarreled with your father in the days preceding his death?"

A: "Yes."

Q: "Will you please describe the nature of your disagreement?"

I held my breath. Although Sir Albert had been told the full story of Alan's conflict with Max, I had asked him to avoid the precise subject if possible. He agreed, with the proviso that he would use it in the full trial later on if it were needed. Now I saw that Alan had prepared an answer.

A: "Yes, it was about money. He wanted to reduce the allowance given me from my grandfather's trust."

Q: "Now, Mr. Fordham, is it not true that you threatened your father on the evening before his death?"

Alan looked startled, and I realized that of course he did not know that Max had told me of the scene between them.

A: "I was rather angry. I suppose I may have said things I didn't mean."

Q: "Did you in fact raise your arm in a threatening gesture and say to your father, 'I'll kill you if you persist'—or words to that effect?"

A: (looking down and speaking in a low voice): "I don't remember."

Q: "You don't remember? May I suggest that you make an effort to refresh your memory? I shall put the question again, Mr. Fordham. Did you threaten your father on the night before he was killed?"

A: "Perhaps I said something like that, but of course I didn't mean it literally."

Q: "You didn't mean it literally!" Sir Albert paused dramatically, then shifted to another topic. "You have said that you were acquainted with Miss Winfield. Have you ever visited her at her residence?"

A: "Yes, on one occasion."

Q: "Then you are familiar with the location of her room and the entrance to it from the small street known as Wortle's Lane?"

A: "Yes."

Q: "Now, Mr. Fordham, you acknowledge that you were not on good terms with your father. Yet on the morning of his death you tell us that he was kindly arranging for you to meet an attractive young lady in the near future. Did you not perhaps regard this as a gesture of conciliation on his part?"

A: (angrily) "No! I regarded it as an unwarranted intrusion into my private affairs."

Q: "Mr. Fordham, will you please tell us where you were on the afternoon of the fourteenth of March at approximately four o'clock?"

A: (looking extremely uncomfortable): "Yes. I was at home having tea with my mother."

Q: "Was anyone else present at the time?"

A: "No, the servants had gone out. Mother made the tea herself and we sat in the kitchen."

Q: "Mr. Fordham, I put it to you that at four o'clock on the fourteenth day of March you were not having tea with your mother, that in fact you went to Doughty Street with the intention of visiting Miss Winfield, that you found your father there—having let himself in with Miss Winfield's key which he had inadvertently dropped into his pocket the evening before; that you renewed your quarrel, that your voices were raised, and that you then seized a bronze bust and struck your father a blow on the head. Realizing that he was dead, you then returned home and asked your mother to attest that you were with her at four o'clock."

Mr. Chatterjee arose. "I did not wish to interrupt my learned friend in his dramatic portrayal of a fictional scenario of such imaginative skill. However, I must remind him that this witness does not stand accused in this case."

Sir Albert (with an exquisite gesture of disdain): "That is regrettably so. Thank you, Mr. Fordham."

As Alan turned to leave the witness box, Mr. Chatterjee spoke. "One moment, Mr. Fordham. I have one further question for you. Did you kill your father?"

Alan: "No, I did not."

As Alan stepped down, James came back to speak to me quietly. "Now you can see Sir Albert's style on cross-examination. With a jury he's marvelous. He doesn't rant nor rave, he simply devastates them with that icy look."

2 4

A lan was led out of the courtroom, passing his sister as she was brought in to testify.

When Sheila entered and was led to her place in the witness box, there was a slight stir as her beauty shone in all its radiance in the drab room. Gone were the bizarre garments she had worn on the evening when Patch and I had seen the Fordham family at the opera house. Now Sheila was wearing an exquisite little suit of pale blue wool. The masses of dark brown hair were caught and coiled at the back of her head, while enchanting tendrils artfully framed the flowerlike face. When she took the oath her voice was rich and clear, with the flawless projection that is the gift of the born actress.

Q: "Miss Fordham, can you tell us please of a conversation you held with your father before his death concerning the defendant, Miss Winfield?"

A: "Yes. I asked him if he was in love with her."

Q: "And how did you know of his friendship with Miss Winfield?"

A: "My brother had told me that my father was—well, having an affair with her."

Q: "And what did your father say to you when you inquired about his relationship with the defendant?"

A: "He said that she was merely a friend and not the kind of person he would ever care for seriously. He said that she was jealous and possessive and that he was planning to stop seeing her quite soon."

James turned to look at me and I saw that he recognized the absurdity of Sheila's statement. The question was whether she had invented the conversation or whether Max had indeed said these things to her.

When Sir Albert rose to cross-examine, it was soon clear that he wondered about the same thing.

Sir Albert: "Now, Miss Fordham, when your brother Alan told you that your father was 'having an affair' with the young lady who is the defendant here, were you distressed?"

A: "Not really. I simply didn't believe him."

Q: "You were very fond of your father?"

A: (tears filling the beautiful eyes) "Yes, he was wonderful."

Q: "What is your age, Miss Fordham?"

A: "I am nineteen."

Q: "I see. And your father was extremely fond of you?"

A: "Oh, yes!"

Q: "Then, do you think it is possible that he may have made the statement to you that he did in order to protect you from distress?"

A: (the tears spilling over): "I don't think that Daddy would have lied to me."

Sheila reached down into the handbag that hung over her shoulder, obviously groping for a handkerchief. As she pulled her hand out of the bag a flash of brightly colored fabric could be seen slipping to the floor as Sheila raised a handkerchief to her eyes. A nearby attendant stooped to pick up the fallen object, and as he arose everyone could see that he was holding by the corner a silk scarf with a banded border and bright red figures in the center. Sheila murmured "Thank you" and began to stuff the scarf back into her handbag.

Sir Albert spoke quickly: "Excuse me, Miss Fordham, does the object you are holding belong to you?"

A: (in surprise): "This? Yes."

Q: "May the clerk examine it, please?"

A: (puzzled): "Yes, of course."

The clerk stepped forward, took the scarf, and held it by two corners so that everyone in the courtroom could see the unmistakable pattern of scarlet elephants in the large central area of the scarf. After a moment of stunned silence Sir Albert cleared his throat.

Q: "Miss Fordham, I believe this is what is known as a silk square or scarf, is it not?"

A: "Yes."

Q: "Where did you obtain this scarf?"

A: "Daddy gave it to me at Christmas."

Q: "Do you know where it was purchased?"

A: "Yes, I believe it came from a small boutique in Paris, a shop he was fond of."

Q: "And will you describe how it may be worn?"

A: "Well, it may be tied round the neck or it may be worn on the head. Is that what you mean?"

Q: "Yes, precisely. Have you yourself worn this scarf over your head at any time?"

A: "Yes, certainly."

Q: "Now, Miss Fordham, will you please think carefully before you answer this question, and remember that you are under oath. A witness at this hearing has testified that on the afternoon of your father's death at shortly before half past four o'clock, a young lady wearing upon her head a scarf precisely resembling the one the clerk is holding was seen walking out of a gate adjacent to Miss Winfield's residence, the place where your father's body was found. Miss Fordham, were you there at that time?"

There was a long pause while Sheila absorbed the shock of this revelation and was clearly debating about what reply to make. She would of course never have imagined that Max had given each of us the same scarf as a personal gift.

At last Sheila's initial look of fright gave way and she answered resolutely: "Yes, I was there."

Sensation!

Mr. Chatterjee leaped to his feet. The magistrate bent a gaze of fatherly concern upon Sheila.

Magistrate: "Miss Fordham, I must inform you that you may have a solicitor present and that you need answer no further questions at this time if your answers would tend to incriminate you."

A: (turning to him with a look of melting innocence): "But I am happy to answer the questions. I have nothing to hide!"

Mr. Chatterjee to the Magistrate: "Sir?"

Magistrate (to Sir Albert): "You may proceed."

Sir Albert: "Will you please explain how you happened to be at the defendant's residence on the day in question?"

A: "I wanted to meet her."

Q: "How did you know where she lived?"

A: "My brother told me. He said one could go through the gate at the side and her door was opposite."

Q: "And did you go to her door?"

A: "Yes. I knocked but there was no reply."

Q: "Did you try the door handle to see if the door was unlatched?"

A: (shocked): "Certainly not!"

Q: "And what time was it when this took place?"

A: "Oh, it must have been well after four o'clock. I don't remember to the moment."

Q: "Was it raining at the time you approached the door?"

A: "No, not really. It had been absolutely pouring earlier, but only a light rain was falling at that moment."

Q: "And you had tied this same silk scarf over your head at this time?"

A: "Yes."

Q: "After you had knocked on the door, what occurred next?"

A: "I knocked again, and when there was no reply I went back through the gate."

Q: "Which way did you walk?"

A: "I turned right and walked back to where I had parked my car. There was a large lorry parked in the street, and I had to squeeze round it to get out."

Q: "Now, Miss Fordham, you have testified that your father told you he was planning to terminate his—er—friendship with Miss Winfield. If that is so, why did you wish to see her?"

A: "I suppose I wanted to see what she was like. I told my brother what Daddy had said about her, and Alan laughed and said she wasn't like that at all. He thinks she's simply marvelous. So I wanted to find out for myself. I was sure she was just a schemer and that Alan had been deceived by her."

Q: "Miss Fordham, you have stated that your father described Miss Winfield as, I quote, 'jealous and possessive.' Were those the precise words he used?"

A: (delicate eyebrows drawn together as if in an effort to remember): "Well, perhaps not precisely. I had the impression that that was what he meant."

Q: "I see." Long pause. "Thank you, Miss Fordham. That will be all."

Sir Albert sat down with an air of having made his point.

Sheila was the last witness to be called. When she had been escorted from the courtroom, Sir Albert rose and moved to dismiss the charge against me. He argued vigorously that since the testimony of Miss Leach about my leaving the house at four twenty-five was no longer valid, the case for the Crown was seriously impaired. He also pointed out that either Alan or Sheila could conceivably have committed the crime and that therefore there was reasonable doubt that I was guilty.

Mr. Chatterjee, while acknowledging that Miss Leach's evidence was disproved, argued that although Alan Fordham had a motive for killing his father, the evidence indicated that he was not present at the scene of the crime. On the other hand, Sheila Fordham admitted to being present near the time of the murder but had no motive whatsoever, having been obviously devoted to her father.

In the end the magistrate stated that despite the elimination of Miss Leach's evidence, I could certainly have been in my room at four o'clock, quarreled with Max, struck him, and left the room earlier, unseen by Miss Leach or anyone else. I could then have returned at twenty minutes before five, denying that I had been there earlier. If Alan's alibi could be broken or if new evidence was brought forth, the case might be altered. Barring such contingencies, he saw no valid reason for dropping the charge against me. He pronounced that I would be held for trial on a charge of murder at the Old Bailey, the date to be set according to the calendar of that court.

Then came the argument for extending my freedom on bond, and now it was Mr. Chatterjee who won my undying gratitude by concurring in Sir Albert's request and leaving the decision to the magistrate, who then agreed that I need not be remanded in custody but would be free until the trial, provided I made no effort to leave the jurisdiction of the Court.

Afterward, as I stood with James and Andrew outside the courtroom, I was astonished to see Sir Albert come down the steps toward us, looking positively cheerful.

"My dear Miss Winfield!" he exclaimed. "Splendid, splendid! Once a jury hears that there are others with motive and opportunity to commit this crime, we should be able to rely on the doctrine of reasonable doubt, with very favorable results. In my experience juries are most reluctant to convict when alternate solutions are presented, even if those possibilities are not proven."

On this note Sir Albert took his leave. I tried desperately to share his optimism, but all I could think of was that I was now formally charged with murder. James and Andrew urged me to come out to dinner with them, but the thought of food made me shudder. They left me at my hotel, where I phoned my father and told him what had happened. He insisted that I stay on at the Edgar for the present and tried to sound reassuring. But when I put down the phone, the tears that I had held back for so long came coursing down my cheeks and I threw myself on the bed, sobbing like a child.

2 5

T hat night I lay awake for hours, restless and miserable, my mind going over and over the events of the day. No one had ever held out any hope to me that the charge against me would be dropped. Yet I realized I had subconsciously hoped for a miracle that didn't come. It was fine that Sir Albert was enthusiastic at last, but I felt frustrated because I knew he still did not believe in my innocence and only hoped to throw enough dust in the eyes of a jury that they would let me off. And what if the jury didn't cooperate? There was no guarantee that they would believe me innocent.

Then my thoughts turned to Max and the girl in Paris. What a spoiled child he had been, snatching at whatever pleasures life offered. More than once I had remembered Max's description of his father and had seen the same pattern developing in Max—the obsession with being admired, the inability to tolerate rejection. Everyone must feed his ego in some way. I wondered about Cynthia's account of the girls who threw themselves at Max and became desperate when he tired of them. I could easily believe that Max would have no compassion in such a case. But I also wondered what would happen if someone he cared for had rejected him. I knew that he had rather enjoyed my own casual attitude toward him. But what if I had become interested in someone else? He might have turned rather nasty if he felt that I no longer found him attractive or preferred another man.

I thought again of the hearing that day and of the startling fact that Sheila Fordham had actually been at my door near the time of Max's death. Had she really come earlier than she said, found Max there, quarreled with him, struck him in anger? Suppose Max had taunted her with her naiveté about his affairs? The shock of disillusionment with her adored father might well have roused her to fury. Could she have been there as early as four o'clock, when Mrs. Hall heard the voices, and not departed until twenty-five minutes later, when Miss Leach saw her going out of the gate? But how could it be proved, even if it were true? And would her exasperation with her father cause anger sufficient to strike a fatal blow?

I must at last have drifted off to sleep, for I awoke from a nightmare in which grotesque creatures leered at me, chanting "Guilty, guilty, guilty!"

The next morning my telephone rang, and it was James. "I've just learned that your friend Patch's parents are in town, at Claridge's. Andrew and I thought it would be a good idea for me to talk with them. Do you want to come along?"

"Yes, of course."

I thought of my pleasant visit to Sussex at Christmastime. Certainly, Lady Muriel and Lord Dodson had been delightful to me then, but I was not at all sure how I would be received in the present crisis. I felt awkward about not having mentioned my acquaintance with Max when Lady Muriel had spoken to me about him, but I longed to hear news of Patch.

When James called for me I tried to look as cheerful as possible. "How did you know where to find them?" I asked.

"Actually, last week I had rung up Lord Dodson's place in Surrey and learned that they were due to return from Italy yesterday—the day of your hearing—and would be in London for a few days before going down to the country."

"I wonder if they know about Max's death and what has happened to me? I'm sure they would have written to Patch if they knew."

"Probably not. In any case, we are ostensibly calling on them to inquire about their daughter, but after that episode at the Savoy when Lady Muriel and Max were together, Andrew suggested that I do some fishing."

At Claridge's we were directed to Lord Dodson's suite. He opened the door himself, giving me a little pat on the shoulder and emitting what sounded like sympathetic mutters.

Lady Muriel came toward me, her hand extended. "My dear Jane, this is quite terrible news. We came in last evening from Rome and knew nothing at all of this until we saw the newspaper stories this morning."

A tray with coffee was on a table, and when I had introduced James and we were seated with our cups, Lady Muriel went on. "I wasn't aware that you were acquainted with Maxwell Fordham." She looked at me intently but her tone was casual. "I believe we were speaking of him at Christmas, were we not? Perhaps you had not met him at that time?"

Before I could reply, James intervened, speaking to Lady Muriel. "I believe *you* were acquainted with Mr. Fordham, were you not?"

Lady Muriel gave us a dazzling smile, all sweet innocence. "Oh, yes, but we haven't seen him for simply ages."

Lord Dodson scowled and turned to look out the window, and James went on. "I am hoping to find someone who might have seen Miss Winfield on the afternoon that Mr. Fordham died. I believe that was on the day you left London. Had you come up from the country that day?"

Lady Muriel thought for a moment. "No. I believe we came up on the Wednesday. There was a concert at the Royal Festival Hall that evening that I particularly wanted to attend."

"Then can you tell me at what time you left London on Friday?"

Lady Muriel turned to her husband. "What time was it, do you remember, Dods?"

Lord Dodson continued to gaze out of the window. Then he slowly turned and seemed to awake from a trance. "We were here at the hotel. Took an early evening flight from Heathrow. Must have left here about half past five or so. Would you agree, my dear?"

Lady Muriel nodded. "Oh, yes, about then, I should think. When I came in from shopping Patricia was here. Then you came in and we all left soon after. But I am afraid we did not see Jane at all that day."

"You see," I said, "I went to look for Patch in Charlotte Street at about half past three. I spoke to her landlady, and then I wandered along Tottenham Court Road and into Great Russell Street. If either of you had gone to call for Patch, you might have seen me along the way."

Lady Muriel looked across the room at her husband. "But Patricia came in a taxi, did she not, dear?"

Lord Dodson blinked, then said ponderously, "Yes, I'm sure she did. I was at the bookseller's. Wanted some books to take along to Rome, you know."

Then we talked for a little while about Patch and the success of her tour.

I said, "I had a postcard saying she planned to stay on in Frankfort after the tour. Do you know what day she will be coming back?"

Lady Muriel smiled. "No, not precisely. In about a week, I should think."

"Will you tell her when she arrives what has happened to me? I'd like to see her as soon as I can."

"Of course."

As I thought of Patch I felt my eyes filling with tears and turned away.

James stood up. "If you think of anything at all that could help Jane, I'm sure you will let us know."

Lady Muriel put her hand on my arm, but I noticed that she made no attempt to embrace me. "Yes, indeed. What a dreadful thing, Jane. You have all our sympathy."

Lord Dodson walked with me down the passage to the lift, while Lady Muriel lingered behind, speaking softly to James. It was only much later on that James told me what she had said to him. After asking him about the evidence against me and whether he thought I would be acquitted, she had said, "Poor child! I'm sure she didn't mean to kill him. It must have been an accident. Surely a jury will be sympathetic to her."

When James indignantly asserted his belief in my innocence he met with conventional murmurs which implied that of course as my solicitor he would be expected to take that line.

2 6

The next few days passed slowly for me. I fought hard against the depression that threatened to engulf me, but there seemed little to hope for. It was Tuesday afternoon before I was temporarily roused from my lethargy by the arrival of Andrew Quentin, followed soon after by a surprise visitor.

Andrew had been out of town over Sunday and Monday, and when I inquired if he had had a pleasant journey, he said cryptically, "Yes and no. Actually, I went to Bath, which is always a pleasure. There can't be many lovelier views than the one from the bridge over the river, with the Abbey above and the Avon pouring along over those little weirs or whatever they are."

I smiled. "And those gorgeous buildings, absolutely reeking of Jane Austen. But did you ever taste the medicinal water?"

"Yes, once. Never again."

"Did you find anything useful?" I had assumed that his visit was connected with the article he was writing for the music journal.

He hesitated. "I'm not sure, at this point, whether the trip was a success or not."

Since scholarly research has often been compared to an iceberg—a large part of the material acquired is never used and often only that small percentage at the tip ever makes it into the final product—I was not surprised at his comment. Only a few hours later did I learn the real purpose of his journey to Bath.

Andrew was about to reply when we looked up and saw an extremely pretty blond girl coming into the lounge, where we were the only occupants at that moment.

The girl came toward me. "Are you Jane Winfield? They told me at the desk that you were here. I'm Brenda West. James Hall asked me to come."

I made the introductions and Brenda said to Andrew, "So you are the professor James has been speaking about. I'm glad you're here, as I know he wants you to hear this also. Something has happened that may have a bearing on your case, Jane, and James asked me to come along and tell you about it myself. He's booked up this afternoon and can't get away."

Brenda sat down and took a sheaf of notes from her briefcase. I saw that she was not only lovely to look at but equally bright and competent.

"What happened is that this morning James received a phone call from Detective Chief Inspector Kent, saying that

Sheila Fordham had been brought in to the Hampstead police station for questioning."

I looked up in surprise. "Do you mean she's suspected of murdering her father?"

"No, actually not. That's what James thought for a moment, too. But it seems that a young chap named Rick Benton, who is a member of a rock group called the Mogs, was brought in yesterday on a charge of selling drugs. He finally confessed and implicated his buddy, Fritz Morgan, and Fritz's girlfriend, Sheila Fordham!"

Andrew looked thoughtful. "I wonder if this has something to do with those trips to New York the two of them were making."

"Yes, it does. Here's what happened. When Sheila was brought in, the Scotland Yard detective who was questioning her learned that she was the daughter of the murder victim, Maxwell Fordham, and he immediately called in Inspector Kent, who is of course leading that investigation, in case there should prove to be a connection with the Fordham case.

"It appears that Sheila was cautioned and told that she might have a solicitor present, but, just as she did at your hearing, she insisted that she had nothing to hide. Rick Benton, Fritz's pal, had told the police that on three occasions he had gone to the Fordham home and picked up various zipper bags or carryalls from Sheila that Fritz had directed her to give to Rick when he called for them.

"Sheila's story is that each time she and Fritz went to New York for her screen tests it happened that he did not come back with her, saying that he had unfinished business in New York. Each time he asked her to bring back some of his gear. He said it was music for his group and that his friend Rick would pick it up from her. She claimed at first that she had no idea the bags contained anything other than what Fritz had told her.

"Then Inspector Kent took over the questioning. I have a copy here of the interview, which was taped and transcribed this morning."

I was astonished. "Inspector Kent gave this to you?"

"Yes. In fact, he told me to tell you, Jane, that Scotland Yard has no desire to convict the wrong person. If any evidence appears that might even remotely help you, he wants your solicitor to have it."

Brenda sifted through the papers in her hand.

"Here is where the important part begins. As you will see, Sheila apparently couldn't resist making the most of a dramatic situation. She isn't in drama school for nothing!" And Brenda proceeded to read to us from the transcript.

Inspector Kent: "Now, Miss Fordham, can you tell me please what has been your relationship with Mr. Frederick Morgan, known as 'Fritz'?"

A: "Yes. We were very much in love."

Q: "I see. And are you aware that Mr. Morgan has told the police that you *were* aware of the illegal contents of the bags you turned over to Mr. Rick Benton?"

A: "Fritz said that? Did he say I knew all along or only—"

Q: "He said that you may have known all along but that on the third occasion you most certainly were aware of the contents of the bag."

A: "But has he admitted—I mean, why would he tell you this at all?"

Q: "You see, Miss Fordham, we have three bags in our possession, all indicating the presence of illegal substances in the linings of certain pockets. On the straps of the bags we found the baggage tags containing flight numbers and have ascertained that those were the flights on which you traveled."

A: "Why didn't they throw away the tags?"

Q: "It is not for me to say. It certainly appears that it would have been to their advantage to do so. In the light of this and other evidence, Mr. Morgan has taken the wise course of admitting his actions. Do you still wish to maintain that you knew nothing about the presence of the drugs?"

A: "I don't know—"

Q: "Miss Fordham, if you will tell us the full truth now, it may be very much to your advantage. Do you still care enough for Mr. Morgan to risk serving a prison term in order to protect him?"

A: "No, I certainly don't! I'll tell you just what happened. It was after the third time I came back from New York. I was sitting there looking at Fritz's bag and decided to open it. I don't know why—just idle curiosity. At first I thought there was only music in it, but then I noticed something bulky in a side compartment and found that it held packets filled with white powder. Of course I was afraid it was drugs and I was horrified. When Rick came to pick up the bag I just gave it to him and didn't say a word, but when Fritz returned I told him what I had found and said I would never do anything like that again. He just laughed and said I was being silly, that everyone did it. He said they would never suspect me because I didn't fit the profile, whatever that is. But I was furious and he finally agreed that he would never ask me to help him again."

Q: "Did you not realize that it was your duty to report this to the police?"

A: "That was the big problem. How could I possibly tell you people about this? Fritz and I were in love. But then I was terribly frightened. I knew that if they were caught I might be involved and go to prison or something. I was afraid Rick Benton would tell about picking up the bags

from me—and you see, that's just what has happened.
But I never believed that Fritz would tell about me. I
thought he would try to protect me."

Q: "Did you tell anyone else about this?"

A: "Well, at first I thought about telling my brother, Alan,
but he had been dreadfully upset about—well, about his
own affairs, and besides I didn't see that he could do
much to help. Finally I decided to tell Daddy about it, so
I did, on the afternoon of the very day that he—that he—
died. I told him the whole story, and he was absolutely
furious. He said that I was never to see Fritz again. Well,
of course I couldn't stop seeing Fritz. After all, we were
in love. Then it got worse. Daddy swore that he would
turn Fritz in to the police and that I would be all right
because I would testify against him. We quarreled desperately about it.

"I was so upset I didn't know what to do. I begged him
to wait and think things over. He was standing there with
some keys in his hand and he kept turning them over and
over. Finally he looked down at the keys and said, 'I must
see Jane. I must return her keys.' And he went out.

"I rang up Fritz right away and told him what happened. Fritz knew all about Jane because Alan had told
me she was Daddy's girlfriend, and I had told Fritz. Then
I paced around for a bit trying to think what to do. After a
while I thought, Daddy's going to tell Jane about this.
Maybe she will help me. Alan said she had been very
decent to him and tried to help him with Daddy. So I
popped into my car and went round to her place. I
thought I would see Daddy's car but there was a huge
lorry in the side street sort of blocking everything.

"Then I went up to Jane's door and knocked and there
was no answer, so I came away. It was just as I said at
Jane's hearing."

Q: "Miss Fordham, may I point out to you that this is not precisely the same story that you told at Miss Winfield's hearing?"

A: "Well, what I *did* is the same, isn't it? Naturally I couldn't say all about Fritz then, could I?"

Brenda laid the papers down on the table. "There's more, of course, but mostly they go back over the same ground. Inspector Kent told me that they decided to let Sheila go for the present, since their chief goal is to convict Fritz and his chum Rick. She will be called as a witness against them and seems quite willing to testify, now that she is disenchanted with her friend. Of course, what's important for you, Jane, is that little Sheila has provided herself with a first-rate motive for killing precious Daddy."

"Yes, I see that. Even if she didn't do it, it certainly will give Sir Albert more ammunition at the trial."

Andrew nodded. "The magistrate at your hearing gave as two of his reasons for not dropping the charges against you that Alan had an alibi and that Sheila had no motive. Now at least one of those conditions is met."

We all sat in silence for a few moments, thinking of the implications of Sheila's statements on the transcript. Suddenly a beautiful sound floated out in the air, a fragment of something from Mozart, although I couldn't remember what. I realized that it was Andrew, softly whistling and evidently quite unconscious of what he was doing. Brenda and I exchanged a smile.

The whistling stopped as abruptly as it had begun and Andrew murmured, "Hmm, well—" as if awaking from a trance, and presently he bid us good-bye.

As Brenda lingered for a moment to gather up her papers and put them away in her briefcase, I asked her if she enjoyed her legal studies.

Her face lighted up. "Oh, yes, it's absolutely fascinating.

And of course it's marvelous working with James Hall. I was lucky to be assigned to him." As she turned to go, she added, "James will be so happy to see this transcript. He heard the essential points from Inspector Kent but not the details. He is most concerned about your case, Jane—as we all are!"

Back in my room, I thought about Brenda West. It was she who had been given extra work during the weeks preceding my hearing and whom James had treated to dinner as a reward. If anyone could help James forget his past love, it would be this lovely young woman. I felt a twinge of pain. How badly my own relationships had turned out—first Brian and then Max! I could at least try to be glad for James's happiness. Surely no one deserved it more.

2 7

S eeking distraction from my unhappy thoughts, I picked up the copy of *Apollo* that had been lying on the table in my room under assorted other items and had now surfaced. Remembering that I had laid it aside that day long ago when James first brought me my mail from Doughty Street, I turned again to the column printed under Max's name.

"On Wednesday evening at the Royal Festival Hall," I read, "the London Symphony Orchestra gave audiences a welcome introduction to the work of Ivan Blenkov, disciple of Polish composer Anton Lenski. In the brief but pungent 'Patterns,' Blenkov displayed inventive configurations within the twelve-tone scale, punctuated with splendid percussive effects. Listeners who expect this music to sound grateful to the ear will inevitably be disappointed. The contemporary composer must be heard on his own terms, not on those of the past, and Blenkov promises to play a major role in the new *avant garde*."

Patch isn't the only one who holds these views, I thought with some amusement. I began to wonder who had done this piece for Max. Perhaps someone on the magazine staff had seized the opportunity to tweak his nose by expressing views contrary to Max's usual line.

As I put the magazine down, I was surprised to hear a knock on my door. I hadn't yet ordered my tea, and the maids were seen only in the mornings.

"Who is it?" I called.

"It's me, Janie. Brian."

Oh, no. Not Brian.

Reluctantly I opened the door and Brian pushed past me, closing the door behind him.

"How did you get here?"

"Easy. I know your room number, so I just walked up the stairs and found your room. Come on, Janie, you're not going to give me that British propriety stuff, are you?"

"No," I said wearily. "I don't care. Sit down."

"I don't want to sit down!"

Then I noticed that Brian was angry.

"What's the trouble?"

"I'll tell you what's the trouble! I don't like you sending people out to spy on me!"

"What do you mean?"

"As if you didn't know. First your lawyer—that James Hall—comes snooping around, looking at my passport and all that. Now your handsome professor chases me all over England."

"Brian, I really don't know what you are talking about."

"OK, I believe you. Well, your precious Dr. Quentin

came down to Bath the other day, where I was staying while I looked up some descendants of my emigrant group, and really gave me the third degree about where I was on the day your famous lover was murdered. It seems Dr. Q had gone to Bristol first and checked up on when I arrived at the hotel there that night. Of course he couldn't prove anything. I checked in about eight thirty, so he pointed out—ever so politely, of course—that I could have been in London at four o'clock."

I looked straight into his eyes. "And were you in London at four o'clock?"

Brian dropped all the indignation and gave me his best little-boy look. "No, Janie, really and truly, I was on the train, as I told you before."

Brian was never more earnest than when he was lying, as I knew from bitter experience, but he could also be telling the truth. Sometimes it was impossible to know.

We were still standing facing each other, and suddenly Brian took one step forward and I found myself in his arms, his face buried in my neck. "Oh, God, Janie, I've missed you!"

He kissed me gently, then more passionately, and I felt as if I were floating slowly downward, like Alice down the rabbit hole. Of course I knew I could never rely on Brian, but what did it matter if this didn't last? It was heavenly to have his arms around me, to feel for a little while at least that I was loved. I had tried so desperately to keep up my courage through the ordeal of the murder. Now all I wanted was to give up the struggle, to stop fighting, to find whatever peace and comfort came my way.

I pulled back and looked into his face, my eyes misting over from the sheer sense of relief at giving in to weakness at last, and what I saw was a gleam of triumph in Brian's eyes. It acted on me like an electric shock. A wave of self-loathing swept over me, and I stepped straight to the door and opened it wide.

"Please, just go," I said.

Brian must have seen my revulsion for, to my surprise, he paused for a moment and then muttered, "OK, have it your own way," and strode out the door.

I was still shaken and trembling from Brian's visit when the phone rang.

"Jane Winfield?" said a voice I didn't recognize. "This is Jeremy Welch. I met you with Alan Fordham one day at lunch."

"Oh, yes, Jeremy, I remember you very well."

"Look, Jane, I must talk to you. Can you possibly meet me somewhere?"

"Of course. Where are you?"

"Actually, I'm at the Nag's Head near the Opera House. Do you know it?"

"Yes, I do. I'll be there in ten minutes."

I wondered what on earth Jeremy wanted to see me about, but I welcomed the distraction after my encounter with Brian. When I reached the pub, I found Jeremy waiting, his face pale behind the dark beard. When he had fetched our drinks, he worked his way through the crowd and came back to where I stood against the wall. I thought he probably wanted to talk with me about his relationship with Alan, but in fact he told me the last thing in the world I expected to hear.

"Do you know," Jeremy began, "that I've scarcely seen Alan since the day his father was killed?"

"No. Is something wrong between you?"

"No, it isn't that. He has literally been away. After his father's death, both Alan and his mother were questioned about their movements at the time, as you know. Immediately afterward, Cynthia sent Alan over to Paris to look after the rather complicated matters connected with his father's estate. He came back here for your hearing because he had been called as a witness. Now his mother has shipped him back to Paris again, simply to keep him out of London."

"Why does she want him away?"

"Because she knows Alan was not at home with her at the time of the murder!"

"What!" My heart gave a great leap. "Then she is lying to protect him?"

"Apparently so."

"But, Jeremy, how do you know this?"

"That's what I want to tell you, Jane. I'm simply desperate. It's so awful—I didn't know what to do or where to turn."

Just then two people sitting nearby got up to leave the pub and Jeremy and I slipped into their seats, putting our drinks on the tiny round table beside us. He leaned toward me, his voice shaking and his face distraught.

"Here's what happened. On the night of the murder Alan came to my place and told me that his father had been found dead in your room in Doughty Street. He had told me the evening before about his quarrel with his father, when he had actually threatened him with violence if he didn't relent about the money."

"Yes, Max told me about it that same evening."

"Oh, of course. That's how your barrister knew about it when he questioned Alan at the hearing."

"Yes."

"Well, then, I simply asked Alan outright where he had been that afternoon and he told me he was at home having tea with his mother. But then he refused to say another word about it. The thing is, Jane, I felt at the time that he wasn't telling the truth. I know Alan so well, and he's absolutely no good at lying."

"I felt the same thing, Jeremy, and, oddly enough, so did Inspector Kent. But there was nothing he could do."

"Exactly. Besides, as you may well imagine, I didn't want to believe this of Alan, so I just sort of buried the thought. While he was away in Paris, I had some brief notes from him about what he was doing there, but he made no mention of the murder. Then came the day of your hearing." Jeremy took a deep breath. "It's so difficult to talk about this, Jane."

"Yes, I understand. What happened?"

"Well, after the hearing Alan had promised to let me know the outcome. When he arrived at my place he was extremely upset. He told me that you had been committed for trial at the Old Bailey, and he said, 'It's awful! I had hoped so much that the magistrate would drop the charges against Jane.' Then he said he had to go back to Paris the next day."

"Is there really that much for him to do there?"

"No, I don't think so. That's when I began to realize that something was dreadfully wrong. So I took the plunge and said to him, 'Alan, tell me the truth. Were you really at home with your mother that day?' and he buried his face in his hands and said, 'No, no, I wasn't, but I can't talk about it.'"

"Did he explain?"

"No. I was horrified, and I said, 'Are you just going to stand by and let this happen to Jane?' and he sort of moaned and said that if things went badly for you at your trial, he would come forward. He left the next morning for Paris without saying another word about the murder."

"This is what I've half suspected all along, Jeremy, but I couldn't believe it of Alan."

"Nor could I." Jeremy shook his head. "I've gone over and over it in my mind for days, and today I decided that I couldn't keep silent about it any longer. Not only for you, Jane, although that is vitally important, but actually for Alan himself. I believe that it's better for him in the end if he tells the truth now. If he lets you go to trial and even perhaps be convicted of this crime and if he then confesses, it will look even worse for him than if he admits everything now."

"Of course, he is probably hoping that I will be acquitted."

"Yes, but what an ordeal for you meanwhile. It's wrong, it's wrong, and I simply can't let it go on. But I couldn't bear to go directly to the police, so I decided to tell you."

"Thank you, Jeremy. I think it's best if I call my solicitor now. Are you willing to tell him what you have just told me?"

"Yes."

When I rang James at home, I tried to sound calm, but he was so tremendously excited that I felt my heart beating with wild hope. "You and Jeremy stay right where you are, Jane. I'm coming straight over."

When he arrived, he announced that he had been on to Inspector Kent and that he was to bring Jeremy into the police station at once, where his statement could be taken. Poor Jeremy went along, pitifully distressed but firmly resolved that he was taking the right course.

Later that evening James rang me up to report that everything had gone well. When he and Jeremy reached the station, Inspector Kent had already rung up Alan in Paris—Alan had been asked to record his whereabouts with the police before being permitted to leave the country—and he agreed to return at once.

"At least he is coming back voluntarily," Inspector Kent had said to James. "If we had had to request extradition it might have taken some time."

"I think we have the answer at last, Jane." James's voice was elated. "Once Alan knows that his alibi is broken, the inspector believes that he will tell all. And I'm sure he's right!"

"Yes, I think so too."

James added that he had rung up Andrew Quentin to tell him the good news but learned that he was out for the evening. "I left a message with his friend at the flat."

"Thank you, James." I felt my voice wavering. "I can't tell you how grateful I am for all you've done."

"No thanks needed, Jane," he said gently. "The great thing is that you will be cleared."

Earlier that evening, after James had left the pub with Jeremy, I had discovered that for the first time in weeks I was genuinely hungry. After eating an enormous plateful of food, downed with a second mug of lager, I had walked back to the Edgar in a cloud of exhilaration.

Now, after James's phone call, I tried vainly to get to sleep but I could think of nothing but Alan Fordham and his treachery. It was easy enough to believe that Alan had come to my room that day, found Max there, and struck him in anger, not intending to kill but just seizing the nearest object and striking out in frustration. But how could he stand by and see me falsely accused?

How little we can know people after all, I thought. For all his gentleness and sensitivity, Alan must be a far weaker person than I imagined. Certainly knowing that you have killed someone, even if unintentionally, must be terribly frightening. When Alan saw that I was accused, he must have found it tempting to wait for the outcome before admitting his own guilt. If I were acquitted, then no one need ever know the truth. He must have been encouraged also by his mother's insistence that I would be let off by a sympathetic jury.

Yet I would not have believed Alan capable of such dishonesty. Nor would Jeremy, apparently. Nevertheless, I sensed that James was right and that Alan would now break under pressure, and at last I fell into a deep and refreshing sleep such as I had not known since the day I had found Max's body lying on the floor of my room.

28

T he next morning I was finishing my breakfast at the hotel when I looked up to see walking toward me the last person in the world I would have expected to be there. It was Alan Fordham himself.

He sat down and took my hand in both of his. "Jane, what can I say? It's all been so dreadful. I knew what I was doing to you, but I couldn't help it."

He looked so distressed that I felt a flash of pity for him in spite of my anger. There were still a few people at other tables in the dining room, but Alan was oblivious to his surroundings and plunged on.

"I just came in from Heathrow. I took an early morning flight from Paris and I'm on my way to the police station. I'm to meet Inspector Kent there at ten o'clock. But I had to come to see you first."

"You know then what Jeremy has revealed?"

"Yes, the inspector told me. Poor Jer—I don't blame him. He thought he was acting for the best."

"But, Alan, tell me what really happened about the—that is, about Max." I couldn't quite say the word "murder."

"Yes. I'll tell you the whole story. On the day of Father's death I didn't get home until shortly after six o'clock. Mother was at home alone. The servants were out and Sheila had gone to spend the night with a girlfriend while Fritz and his group were out doing a gig somewhere. Mother told me that a police officer had been there only a few minutes earlier to tell her that Father was dead. He had been found in a house in Doughty Street in a room occupied by a Miss Jane Winfield. He had died as a result of being struck on the head by a heavy object. Apparently this had happened at about four o'clock or after.

"Mother asked me where I had been that afternoon. I told her that I had driven into Hertfordshire to look up a friend and when no one was at home I had simply driven back again. She asked if I had seen or talked to anyone and I said no. She sat very still for a moment or two. Then she asked me to come to the kitchen with her.

"In the kitchen she put the kettle on for tea. Her hands were shaking as she set out the cups. She put out the milk and sugar, and when the tea was ready she poured for both of us. Then she looked at me very earnestly and said, 'Alan, do you see these tea things? We were here together today at four o'clock, drinking tea like this. You must positively swear to this, and I will do the same.'

"Of course I told her that I would. It was awful. She kept avoiding my eye. For the next few days there was a lot of confusion. Mother had to go to identify the body. I offered to go for her but she became quite perturbed and insisted that she go herself. Then there was Sheila to cope with. Poor infant, she took Father's death very badly. I had fetched her from her friend's house that evening and we had to have the doctor for her.

"Then your solicitor, Mr. Hall, talked to Mother and later to me, and it was obvious that he didn't believe my story. When Inspector Kent questioned both of us separately about the events of that day, Mother was dreadfully nervous. Soon after that she sent me off to look after the family financial affairs. I believe she was afraid that I would break down and tell the truth."

I said, "Tell the truth? That you had killed your father?"

Alan looked at me in total disbelief. "That *I* did? No, of course not. That *she* did! Poor Mother, she had every reason to be furious with him. She wanted to be free to marry Hugh, who is an extremely decent chap, and Father, after all his own appalling behavior, was refusing to settle things fairly with her. She knew about you, Jane, and where you lived, because I had told her about seeing you and how wonderful you were. So I realized that she must have gone to your place and found him there, and—well, they must have quarreled and she simply picked up the nearest thing and conked him with it.

"You see, it was obviously an accident. I'm sure she had no idea he was dead until the police came to tell her. It must have been a dreadful shock for her. At first I was perfectly willing to go along with her story of our having tea together at the time of the murder. Then when I learned that you were arrested, Jane, I was pretty upset but Mother kept assuring me that you would get off. I decided to wait at least until your hearing last Friday, hoping that the charges against you would be dropped. But now I can't cope with it any longer. I broke down and admitted to Jeremy that I wasn't really there

having tea with Mother that day. I'm glad Jeremy told you
about it at last."

"But Alan, didn't you realize that we all thought you were
guilty of the murder yourself, not your mother?"

"Oh, lord! You mean all that nonsense your barrister threw
at me at your hearing? I thought that was all window-dress-
ing. You see, I knew I hadn't done it, so I suppose it never
occurred to me that it wasn't obvious to everyone else."

I looked at him with compassion. "I see now why it was so
difficult for you to exonerate me."

"Poor Jane! The whole thing has been an absolute nightmare. I must go now. I'm frightfully worried about Mother. I
hope the police will understand that it was only an accident
and will be lenient with her."

When Alan had gone I called James at once to tell him
about this extraordinary development, and he insisted that I
meet him for lunch so that he could hear the full story.

Then Andrew Quentin called. He had received James's
message about Alan's "confession" and expressed his joy that
now the charges against me would probably be dropped very
soon.

When I told him of Alan's visit and his revelations about
Cynthia Fordham, Andrew was both startled and amused.

"I must say, Jane, that that is a resolution that had never
occurred to me. I'm afraid I'm not living up to your flattering
image of me as a super-sleuth."

I asked him to join us for lunch but he declined, having a
full schedule for the rest of the day.

James had chosen a little French restaurant in the West
End for our luncheon.

"Isn't this awfully expensive?" I murmured when we had
taken our seats.

"My dear girl, money is no object. This is a celebration!"

Over a bottle of wine and the excellent food we talked over every aspect of the dramatic developments of the last few days.

"Poor Alan!" I said. "You must admit that it was a terrible dilemma for him. In order to free me he must incriminate his own mother. What will happen to Cynthia now?"

"What happens to dear Cynthia is that Inspector Kent will bring her in for questioning and once she realizes that Alan no longer supports her story, she may break down and confess. Even if she doesn't, there will be a strong circumstantial case against her. She has an obvious motive, and the fact that she committed perjury at your hearing will not make things look any better for her. We have excellent grounds for dismissing the charge against you."

"Poor Cynthia!"

James's blue eyes sparked with anger. "I must say, Jane, that I don't feel much sympathy for her when she was so willing to let you be the fall guy for her."

"Still, it is a sad thing for the whole family, isn't it?"

James suddenly lost his look of anger. "Yes, of course it is. I didn't mean to sound like the Avenging Fury. It's just that it has been pretty hard on you."

I smiled. "I'm all right now."

Then we talked about Sheila and Fritz and the drug charges against them.

"Will they be lenient with Sheila?" I asked.

"Oh, they will undoubtedly let her off if she testifies against Fritz and his chum, as evidently she will."

"What about Fritz? If this is a first offense, might he be given probation?"

"But it isn't a first offense. I learned from Inspector Kent that this is his second violation. The first occurred more than a year ago, before he and Sheila met, and she knew nothing about it. He is out on bail now, but young Fritz is in pretty

serious trouble. Fortunately for him, his family have money.
He's going to need it."

I remembered that it was Brenda West who had brought
me the transcript of Sheila's interview with the police.

"Brenda seems very competent," I said.

James beamed. "Yes, she's splendid, isn't she? She's making excellent progress."

I could see the pride glowing in his face and felt a quick
hot thrust of pain that I couldn't control. Ever since my
meeting with Brenda I had tried desperately to be glad that
James had found such a lovely girl. Now, looking at him
across the table, I knew beyond any doubt that this was the
man I could have loved with all my heart. Why hadn't I
realized it long ago, before it was too late?

29

L ater that afternoon I had a phone call from Andrew Quentin at my hotel.

"Jane, I have something to tell you. After you told me this morning about Alan Fordham's statement that he hadn't killed his father, I got to thinking about the whole thing and had a sort of hunch. So I made a long-distance phone call. Will you be there about seven o'clock this evening?"

"Yes. But why?"

Andrew hesitated. "I want you to be prepared for a visitor."

"All right. But what is it all about?"

He paused again. "I don't mean to sound evasive, but I can't really say anything more just now." And he rang off.

At a few minutes before seven I went down to the television lounge and sat where I could see anyone who entered the hotel. I may as well see who my mystery visitor is, I thought.

A news program ended and as someone in the lounge got up to switch to another channel, I saw a taxi drive up and a young woman with reddish hair descend, carrying a backpack. Then she paid the driver and lifted out a large object that looked for all the world like a cello case.

I leaped to my feet. "Patch!"

"Hello, Jane."

"Come up to my room." I took the cello from her and led the way to the lift.

"I've just come in from Frankfort and I came straight here to see you."

I was so overjoyed to see Patch that I didn't bother to wonder why she hadn't gone to her own place first to deposit her things or how she knew where to find me.

Then I remembered that I was expecting a visitor. As I settled Patch into a chair in my room, I said, "Look, I think someone's coming along shortly. Do you remember my professor, Dr. Quentin?"

"Yes, of course. We met one day when he first came to London."

I told her all about Andrew and his cryptic announcement that someone would be there soon.

To my astonishment she said, "Yes, I know. I'm the someone!"

It was then I noticed for the first time that Patch's face was chalk white, the freckles standing out starkly through the pallor.

"Patch! What is it?"

"Oh, Jane, it's so dreadful. I had no idea until this morning that Maxwell Fordham was dead. I still can't believe it. And then to find out that you were accused of the murder—"

"But it's all right now, Patch. You see, they know now that I didn't kill Max."

Patch looked at me strangely. "But of course you didn't, Jane. I know that better than anyone because I killed him myself!"

I stared at Patch in utter disbelief. Patch? But how? Why?

"When Dr. Quentin phoned me in Frankfort this morning, he asked me first if I knew about Max's death and I told him I had heard nothing about it. Then he told me that Max had been found in your room on the afternoon of the day I left for the Continent, and that you had been charged with the crime. He asked me quite simply if I had been there that day. I told him at once that I had been there and asked him to let me tell you about it myself. He agreed and told me that I would find you here at the Edgar."

"Your mother hadn't told you that I was accused of murder? I saw her on Saturday."

"No. I haven't talked with her since Friday evening, when they first returned from Italy. Knowing Mimi, I can guess that she knew I would be concerned about you and wanted to spare me until I came home. Of course she would have no idea that I knew anything about Max's death."

"But Patch, I can't believe it! What on earth happened that day?"

And then she told me her story.

"On the day I left for the Continent," Patch began, "I took a taxi from my place in Charlotte Street at about three o'clock to Claridge's, where I was to meet Mimi and Dods for our flight from Heathrow. They were going with me to Frankfort for the first concert of the tour and then on to Florence and Rome. When I arrived at the hotel they were both out, and after mooching about for a time I decided on the spur of the moment to pop into a taxi and go round to say good-bye to you. It must have been shortly before four o'clock or so when I came to your door. I let the taxi go, thinking that if you were not at home I would walk a bit and find another.

"When I knocked, I was astonished to see Maxwell Fordham open the door. We stared at each other in mutual surprise. Then he asked me to come in and explained that he had come to return your keys and was waiting for you to come home. He told me that he had been seeing you for several months, and, knowing Max, I assumed that you had been lovers. You see, a year ago in the summer—" For the first time the pallor in Patch's face gave way and a deep flush suffused her countenance. "I think I told you there was someone—"

"Do you mean it was Max? I thought it was your friend Jeremy!"

"Jeremy Welch? Oh, no. Jeremy is a dear and I'm terribly fond of him, but not in that way. Nor would he be—I mean—"

"Yes, I know."

"Oh, of course, you must know about Jeremy and Alan. In fact, it was concerning that relationship that I had seen Max only the week before I left on the tour. Until then I hadn't heard from him at all since—what does one say—the end of the affair?"

My heart went out to Patch. "Did you care very much for him?"

"Oh, quite desperately at first. I was at the gatehouse in the late summer while Mimi and Dods were away, and Max began dropping in rather often. He told me that his wife had a lover and he was feeling lonely and at loose ends. He began making love to me quite soon and I was simply wild with joy. Except for one or two fleeting and rather unsatisfactory affairs, I had never been in love before. The odd thing is, Jane, that I didn't for a moment expect it to last long, and when it ended I was devastated but not at all surprised.

"By the end of the summer I sensed that Max was cooling, and when I went back to London in the autumn I knew that for him it had been a passing thing and that I would not see him again. For a long time I felt a dreadful sense of loss, of emptiness, but it never occurred to me to seek him out or to make any effort to pursue him. It was over and that was the end of it.

"You can imagine then how surprised I was when I received a note from him a week or so before I left for the tour, asking me to meet him one evening for drinks. He greeted me exactly as if we had parted the day before and began explaining at once his distress over Alan. He knew that Jeremy and I were friends, you see, and he wanted me to tell him everything I could about Jeremy, evidently in the hope that he might somehow break up their relationship. I told him that I thought they had every right to lead their own lives in any way they wished, and he became positively livid and launched into a long tirade about young people today having no standards—"

"I know. I heard the same thing."

"Yes, I can imagine! Well, he must have seen that I was not going to be much help to him in his vendetta against Alan so, incredible as it may seem, he decided to make use of me in another way. He asked me to do a review for him on the Wednesday of the following week because he would be out of town on the night in question. I had done one for him in the summer when our romance was on and I remembered being terribly flattered at the time that he would trust me to do it for him. Now I asked what was on the program and when he told me that the opening number was something of Blenkov's—as you know, he's a disciple of Anton Lenski—I instantly decided to take it on and try to embarrass him by giving my own opinion in the column. I daresay it was absurd, but the idea of creating a small tempest for him was too tempting.

"I've seen the column," I broke in, "and I wondered who had written it. It sounded like your views, all right, but it never occurred to me that it could have been you who did it. Max would have been furious if he had seen it—"

I stopped abruptly and Patch and I looked at each other in mutual anguish at the horror of the situation. Maxwell Fordham was dead and somehow Patch was responsible.

"Oh, Patch, what was it? What happened that day in my room?"

"Well, I told Max that I had done the review and left it at the *Apollo* office, but he didn't seem to be listening. I turned to go and he suddenly looked at me oddly and then referred for the first time to our past encounter. 'You're a cool one,' he said. 'Didn't you miss me last year?' I glared at him and suddenly his face took on a sort of sneer and he said, 'You are an altogether different proposition from your mother.' I asked him what on earth he meant by that. I knew vaguely that he and Mimi had seen a lot of each other after my father died, but I was away at school most of the time. 'Didn't you know we were lovers?' he asked me.

"And then—oh, Jane, he started saying dreadful things about Mimi, that she had been absolutely mad about him and that when he tried to break off she had wept and begged him not to leave her. He said that she married Dods only because she could not have Max.

"Then he went on. 'She rang me up a few weeks ago and asked me to meet her for lunch at the Savoy. That used to be our favorite meeting place. She claimed that she merely wanted to return some jewelry I had given her, but in fact I know she wanted to start seeing me again. I notice that His Lordship whisked her off to Italy soon afterward.'

"I told him that I didn't want to hear any more and he laughed and said that he had only made love to me because it amused him to make love to Mimi's daughter. I didn't mind that for myself but I couldn't bear to hear him talk about Mimi in that dreadful way.

"He began telling me that Mimi was insatiable and that her demands had exhausted him. It was appalling—his voice kept rising and his eyes glittered in a sort of manic way. I turned to go but he reached out and clutched my arm. I pushed him back, and a piece of your manuscript music fell to the floor. Max knelt down to pick up the sheet, and while he was still on his knees he looked up at me and positively hissed, 'Your dear sweet Mimi is nothing but a little slut.' And he started laughing.

"Your bronze bust of Chopin was standing at my elbow and I was so angry I simply picked it up and brought it down on his head. I desperately wanted to hurt him, to make him stop saying those foul things."

"But Patch, why didn't the police find your fingerprints on the bust?"

She looked at me blankly. "Didn't they?" Then her face cleared. "Oh, I suppose I had never taken off my gloves. It was a cold day, wasn't it? I seem to remember stuffing my cap into my coat pocket, but I'm sure I still had my gloves on."

Then she frowned again. "But Jane, this is the part I cannot understand. Max was certainly not dead when I left him. He was not even unconscious. He sort of fell half over, with his head against the sofa, and looked at me reproachfully. Then he said something like 'That hurt—why did you do that?' I was so furious that I muttered, 'Serves you damn well right,' or words to that effect, and stalked out. It was pouring buckets but I was so angry that I went along Doughty Street and was into Theobalds Road before I even bothered to put up my umbrella. I was soaked by the time I found a taxi and went back to the hotel.

"Of course I said nothing to Mimi and Dods about seeing Max. We went off to Frankfort, and once the tour began I put the whole nasty episode out of my mind. I was totally out of touch and knew nothing about Max's death until your professor rang this morning. Good God, Jane, I would never for a single moment have let you go through this ordeal if I had known. It must have been awful for you."

"It's all right, Patch. Of course you didn't know. I think I understand what happened." And then I explained to her what the pathologist had said at the hearing about the kind of injury Max had sustained and how the victim may move about or even speak and then afterward lapse into a coma and die.

"Yes, I see."

"That is what I was told when they believed—that is—"

"Yes, when they believed that you had done it. Poor Jane!"

Then we talked about what Patch should do now. Obviously she had to go to the police, but I persuaded her to tell Mimi first. I was sure that her parents would insist that she have a solicitor with her, and indeed that is what happened. She phoned Mimi at Claridge's and told her briefly what had happened, and in no time at all Mimi and Dods arrived with the family solicitor. We all sat downstairs in the lounge while Patch told her story, suitably editing what Max had said about Mimi but making it clear that he had used insulting language, after which their solicitor went off with Patch to see Inspector Kent.

As Lady Muriel and Dods took their leave, Patch's mother put her arms around me and simply murmured, "My dear Jane!" I knew how distraught she was about Patch, and no other words were needed.

30

E vents connected with the case moved rapidly after Patch had made her statement to the police, but for me, stunned as I was at learning of Patch's involvement in the murder, it was impossible to feel the joy I would otherwise have experienced. When I had believed that either Alan Fordham or his mother had killed Max, I had felt a tremendous surge of relief at being freed from suspicion, but to obtain that freedom at Patch's expense was too painful to allow for much joy.

Patch herself had no such qualms. Her only concern was to tell the whole truth as quickly as possible and to be certain I was cleared. Her very eagerness, however, led to a legal problem which she found exasperating, and so did James. He

reported that when he spoke to Inspector Kent about dropping the charge against me, that good man told him that he
personally believed Patch's story but that before bringing a
formal charge against her, he would like to have some cor-
roborating evidence.

"After all," he said, "people do come in and confess to
crimes they haven't done. And this young lady is a close
friend of Miss Winfield, which makes it all the more suspect."

James declared that he was willing to go before the magistrate on my behalf in any case, when an unexpected development occurred. That very evening at home in Doughty Street
he was chatting with old Mr. Emery, telling him rather
crossly about the circumstances of the case.

"Is Miss Crawford the young lady with the ginger hair?"
Mr. Emery asked.

Surprised, James said, "Yes, she is."

Mr. Emery went on with a benign smile. "I remember her
quite well from last summer. She came into the garden with
Miss Winfield. Plays the cello, does she not? I'm very fond of
cello music."

"Yes. If only someone had seen her hereabouts on the day
of the murder—"

"But I did see her that day! It was nowhere near the house.
It was in Theobalds Road. It must have been about a quarter
past four. There was a very heavy rain and I noticed the
young lady striding rapidly along. What struck me as odd was
that although she was carrying an umbrella, she had not put
it up and she was drenched. Her hair was streaming down
her face and her clothing was soaked. She seemed quite preoccupied, so of course I did not attempt to speak to her."

Dear Mr. Emery! He had not mentioned this before because no one would have supposed that it could bear any

relation to the murder. For all he knew, Patch lived in the neighborhood and was walking along to the shops.

With Mr. Emery's statement, James was able to secure my release from the charge. After the brief hearing before the magistrate, Inspector Kent came to me and shook my hand.

"I'm very glad that we have finally arrived at the truth in this case, Miss Winfield. My instinct from the beginning was to believe your story, but the evidence against you was difficult to refute." He smiled at James. "Mr. Hall here was indeed persistent in declaring your innocence!"

Then the Inspector added, "I thought you both might like to know what happened when I questioned Mrs. Cynthia Fordham."

I had been too much upset about Patch to give a thought to anything else. Now I wondered about Alan's belief that Cynthia had killed Max.

"Yes, please," I said.

"When Mr. Hall first told me young Alan's story, Mrs. Fordham was out of town. We tracked her down and finally brought her in this morning. Her son was called in also, but they had had no opportunity to speak with each other. I had heard the son's story. Now I told his mother that we knew her evidence about their having tea together at the time of the murder was false. She broke down and wept and begged me to understand that she knew her son had killed his father but that it was only an accident and I must understand that there were extenuating circumstances.

"It had never occurred to her that Alan thought *she* had committed the crime. When I brought the two of them together there was a good deal of weeping and mutual explanation, and finally I sent them home, happy but subdued."

Now Patch was duly charged with Max's murder and the newspapers gave the story full spread. Headlines blazed:

PEER'S GRANDDAUGHTER CONFESSES
TO NOCTURNE MURDER

The story appeared on the television news. Although the
family solicitors had tried to shield Patch from publicity, the
news media managed to get pictures of her when she appeared at Magistrate's Court. I was afraid this would be more
painful for Patch than for other less reticent persons, but surprisingly she seemed to be oblivious to the whole procedure.

"I don't care a straw what anyone says," she told me afterward. "So long as you are cleared, Jane, I'll face whatever
happens." She had insisted on pleading guilty and was given
a reduced charge. Now released on bond, she planned to go
home to Surrey in a few days to await her hearing.

After my formal release, my father insisted that I come
home for a rest. "Take at least a month, Jane. You'll need
some time to recuperate from this ordeal."

I hated to leave London before Patch's case was resolved,
but I realized there was nothing I could do to help her and I
thought longingly of the refuge of home. A few days before I
was due to leave, Patch and I had a long lunch, talking over
every aspect of the tragedy that had shaken both our lives. I
told her how Jeremy had feared that Alan was guilty when in
fact Alan thought he was protecting his mother. I could not
mention having seen Lady Muriel's meeting with Max at the
Savoy, but Patch brought up the subject herself.

"You remember all the ghastly things Max said to me that
day about Mimi? Well, I told her everything because Mimi
had to understand why I was so angry with Max. She told me
then that it was utterly untrue, that in fact it was Max who
was infatuated with her after Father died. At first she was

charmed by him, and they became lovers for a time, but she soon realized what a vain and shallow person he was. He wanted to divorce his wife and marry Mimi and when she refused he became nearly deranged.

"Evidently no one Max truly cared for had ever rejected him before, and he simply could not cope with rejection. He begged and pleaded, wept—everything he attributed to Mimi in his tirade to me that day was actually his own behavior. But Mimi broke off with him firmly. By this time she had come to love Dods, and she married him.

"As for their lunch at the Savoy, she *did* phone Max and it *was* to return a ring he had given her which belonged in his family. But it was in response to a note she had had from him asking her to meet him and return the ring. She had tried to return it years before but he had refused to take it then. Now she was afraid he would begin to make a nuisance of himself, but she feared also that an angry response from her would only make him more difficult. So she decided to meet him at the Savoy, as he had suggested. It seems they had gone there often when their romance was on. She gave him the ring, and they talked casually through lunch about their activities in the music world. She's terribly keen on a Young Musicians project just now, and of course she's on the board of several major groups, as you know.

"At the end of the lunch she told him quite calmly but firmly that she was happy now and wished to be let alone. He appeared to accept her at her word that day and promised not to try to see her again.

"Afterward it must have begun to prey on his mind, and on the day I saw him in your room, he had evidently been reliving his feeling of rejection. I suppose that seeing me— Mimi's daughter—triggered a violent reaction."

I said, "It does look as if Max was heading for some sort of emotional breakdown, doesn't it? He told me that his father was very difficult in much the same way. It may have been worse than he admitted. In any case, I am glad to know that Mimi is all right."

"Yes. She has told Dods the whole story, and would you believe it, Jane—Dods actually saw her with Max at the Savoy?"

I looked as blank as possible, and Patch went on.

"Yes. Poor angel, he admitted that he sensed she was hiding something from him that day, so he actually looked in her appointment book and saw *Savoy, one p.m.* It was utterly unlike him to do such a thing, but he told her he has never quite believed his luck in winning her, and after five years he was terrified that she might be growing bored with him. He went to the Savoy that day, feeling that he must know the truth at any cost, and saw her walking out of the dining room with Max.

"Poor darling! He was sick with dread. Mimi said he had been acting quite unlike himself and that's why she suggested the trip to Italy!"

At last Patch and I left the restaurant. Outside, she hailed a taxi and we said a hasty good-bye before either of us should give way to our emotions. I walked quickly away, my head bowed and my eyes stinging with tears.

3 1

O nce I had said good-bye to Patch and sent messages of farewell to Lady Muriel and Lord Dodson, there was little else to do but pack up my things for my return to the States. Andrew Quentin had heartily agreed with my father that I should go home for rest and recuperation.

"Don't even think about Marius Hart unless you feel like it," he advised. "I'll be going back up to Scotland in a few days and then on to the Continent. You can drop me a line and let me know how you are getting on."

James and I had shared with Andrew everything that had happened on the case. Now I asked him about his phone call to Patch in Frankfort. "How did you know that Patch was involved?"

"Oh, I didn't, really. It was just an idea. I'll tell you all about it sometime."

Alan and Jeremy had come to say good-bye, Alan full of apologies and Jeremy sharing with me my concern over Patch. On the day before my departure, I had boxed up assorted kitchen items and other odds and ends which James had taken to his flat to store for me until I should be ready to return to London someday. Although Mrs. Hall had sent a message through James that I might keep my room, we both knew that it would be impossible for me to return to Doughty Street. I dreaded the thought of finding another place. Perhaps this time, I thought, I'll live farther out and simply commute.

At nine o'clock that evening I was getting ready to go to bed early and watch television. I had said good-bye to James when he picked up the boxes, trying desperately to be casual and friendly and to hide the anguish I felt.

Suddenly the phone rang. It was Andrew Quentin, and what he said was so startling that I was shaken out of my depression.

"Hello, Jane. I'm going out to a nightclub and I'd like to take you along! I'd suggest casual clothes. I'll call for you about half past ten."

Andrew at a nightclub? I noticed that he had actually given me no chance to refuse, and I was too curious to dream of not going.

I was wearing pants and a turtleneck sweater under my Burberry when Andrew arrived in a taxi. We drove down into the Strand, past Trafalgar Square, down Whitehall, and then along the Embankment. Presently, somewhere in Chelsea, we arrived at what appeared to be a small private club. Andrew secured our entrance and we descended a narrow flight of stairs and entered a dark and smoke-filled room, where the sound of rock music echoed from the walls while fingers of light flashed and probed in the darkness. From the obscure corner where we sat I saw through the haze that the music proceeded from three guitarists and a drummer, and on the bass drum was inscribed, in mammoth letters, THE MOGS.

Two of the guitar players were singing into their microphones, their bodies gyrating, their voices raucous. I saw that the drummer, with his huge mop of curly black hair, was Sheila's former boyfriend Fritz. As we sipped our drinks, I looked around at the half-filled tables, with people hunched together to talk above the deafening music, or simply sitting and swaying their bodies vaguely to the insistent beat. Andrew was looking slim and attractive in his jeans and a pullover, his fine-featured face keenly alert.

Suddenly I noticed Sheila Fordham at the table next to ours. When I turned to Andrew in surprise, he merely shook his head and indicated silence. I looked at Sheila and was struck again with her dazzling beauty.

When the band reached what seemed to be their final number, we saw Sheila reach into a small cloth bag she was carrying and give the waiter a square of folded paper, saying something I couldn't hear.

At last the music ended to a spattering of applause. In a few moments we saw Fritz make his way through the tables, greeting one or two acquaintances along the way. When he reached Sheila, he stood and looked at her, then roughly pulled her to her feet and kissed her, holding her body tightly and moving his hands down her back to press her against him. Sheila's arms went around his neck and she clung to him, passionately responding to his kiss. Suddenly Fritz pushed her back into her chair.

"So—you're back! I didn't think you'd stay away for good."

Sheila looked at him coolly but with a provocative smile. "Sit down, darling. Have a drink."

Swaying slightly on his feet, Fritz looked down at her. "Sure, OK. Why not?"

He sat down and Sheila bent forward and looked into his face. "Fritz, are you into PCP again?"

"What the hell is it to you what I'm on? Look, Sheel, I've told you before, if you're my girl you don't ask questions. You want to be with me, you take me as I am. Got it?" His head rocked back and he put both hands up, as if to hold his head in place.

Sheila bent toward him again, her voice soft and pleading. "I'm sorry, Fritz. I won't ask again. It's just that you know what it does to you."

"Yeah, OK, forget it."

"Remember the day Daddy was killed. I went to see you after I had gone to Jane's place looking for Daddy. You were really high and that's when you told me what you were taking. You even tried to get me to take some."

"You'd be better off if you weren't so straight. Have a little fun!"

"Did you see in the news that it wasn't Jane who killed Daddy after all?"

"Yeah, I told you that, didn't I?"

"I know you did, but how did you know?"

"Well, I didn't *know*, but I thought it might have been the girl with the ginger hair. Now I see in the papers that she's confessed."

"That's right. You're so clever, Fritz. You were there, weren't you? Is that how you knew?"

Fritz's head swayed forward, then back, and his body twitched. "Sure I was there. I thought I told you that. I saw this tall girl with reddish hair coming out the gate."

"Now that she's confessed, you can tell me all about it. What happened?"

"I went up to Jane's door and it was standing open. The

girl hadn't even bothered to close it. I walked in and there was your dad sitting on the floor rubbing his head. He looked up at me and said, 'You little weasel, what do you think you're doing to my daughter?'

"I said, 'You're not really going to the police. Sheila will be in it up to her neck.'

"And he said, 'Not if she testifies against you.' Then he looked down at a bronze head that was lying on the floor and said, sort of puzzled, 'She hit me with that.' I could see a little bump on his forehead.

"I said, 'OK, have another one on me,' and I picked the thing up and gave him a good crack with it on the same spot." Fritz's voice was beginning to slur. "It's OK to tell you this, Sheel, because I asked a doctor about it, just as a hypotheth—"

"Hypothetical question?"

"Yeah, like that, and he said nobody would be able to tell which blow had caused the blood clot, but he was sure the one who struck first would be blamed. So you see, I'm in the clear, especially since I also wiped that ridiculous bust and everything else clean of my fingerprints."

"Oh, Fritz, you're wonderful," breathed Sheila.

Fritz leaned toward her across the table. "For a straight kid, you're not so bad yourself. Look, have you got any cigarettes?"

He started to reach into Sheila's little cloth bag. She gasped and tried to snatch it out of his hands, and the contents of the bag began to spill out onto the table. A lipstick, mirror, and comb flew out, and then a small flat metal box came out of the bag and lay on the table between them. For one frozen moment Fritz stared. Then comprehension dawned. The object was a tape recorder. Its light was on and the tape inside was moving.

Fritz glared at Sheila and then his arm shot out and he

grabbed her by the hair, while with his other hand he reached for the little tape machine. But Andrew was too quick for him. Deftly, he snatched up the recorder and handed it to me.

"Get back, Jane!" he ordered.

Fritz's reactions were slower, but now a look of insane fury turned his face into a horrifying mask. He dropped Sheila's hair and made a leap for Andrew, getting his hands around his throat and shouting, "You bastard. You set her up. I'll kill you for this!"

Sheila started screaming. "Fritz, don't! Let go! Stop it!"

I looked with terror at the rage in Fritz's face and then I saw a wine bottle on a table nearby. Quickly I snatched it up, turning it upside down to hold it by the neck. With the red wine pouring out over my clothes, I had positioned myself behind Fritz and raised my arm when I heard a voice say, "It's all right, miss. Stand aside, please." The voice held such quiet authority that I instinctively moved away, and the next thing I knew, Fritz was in handcuffs, kicking and thrashing, and Inspector Kent and a constable were hustling him out the door.

In a moment the inspector returned. "He's on the way to the station. We can hold him for his attack on you," he said to Andrew. "Nice work, professor. And you too, Miss Fordham. I'll take this along." And he picked up the tape recorder where I had dropped it on a table. Turning it to OFF, he grinned. "This should fill in the parts we couldn't hear." And he bid us all a cheery good night.

3 2

It was not long past eleven o'clock when Inspector Kent left the club, and half an hour later I found myself sitting with Andrew and James in the flat where Andrew was staying. I had told Andrew firmly that it was high time for him to explain how he had performed his magic tricks, and he had laughingly agreed. He admitted that he had told James he might have a new development in the case, but there was no guarantee that his plan would work. Thus, when Fritz had been despatched to the police station, Andrew had phoned James, told him briefly what had happened, and asked him to meet us at his place.

Meanwhile, at the club, a young man had appeared from a far corner and come to Sheila's side. She presented him to us as her friend Tommy from drama school. "Isn't he divine?" she said. "Whatever did I see in Frightful Fritz?"

Tommy put his arm around her. "How did it go, darling?"

"It was a smash, wasn't it?" she asked Andrew, with a dazzling smile.

"Absolutely first rate! An award-winning performance!"

Sheila turned to me. "When Dr. Quentin asked me if I wanted to do a real-life part, I was thrilled. I knew that if Fritz was high on something, he would babble away at whatever I asked him, and if he actually had hit Daddy that day, I wanted to know about it. I'll never forgive him for that!"

Now, at his flat, Andrew explained that his friend was out of town and we would not be disturbing anyone at this unseemly hour. He handed us drinks, we settled in our chairs, and James said, "Now, Andrew, please begin at the beginning!"

Andrew looked genuinely embarrassed. "I don't pretend to any magic tricks, as Jane called them. Much of what I thought about the case was shared by both of you, I am sure, at one time or another. Then I made some guesses, a few of which turned out to be right.

"When I first came to London on my research leave, Jane told me a good deal about her friends here in London—about Maxwell Fordham and his family, about her friend Patch and her parents, and about you, James, and the people at the house in Doughty Street. Then I went off to Scotland for some time and had just returned to London when I learned that she had been charged with Max's murder.

"Of course, from the beginning, if we assumed Jane's innocence, Alan Fordham was the obvious suspect. He had threatened his father only the evening before, as a culmination to the bitterness that had existed between them for some time. Both of you, and Alan's friend Jeremy, sensed that Alan was lying when he stated that he was having tea with his mother at the time of his father's death. But I confess that I did not suspect that Alan was attempting to protect his mother, believing that she was the culprit.

"Then I began to wonder, as you did, about Jane's former boyfriend Brian. He arrived from the States the day before the murder but lied to Jane and told her that he came in on Sunday. It was only when James happened to see the entry date on Brian's passport that he admitted arriving earlier. He had followed Jane in the fog on that first evening, so he knew where she lived. I wondered if he had lurked about and seen her going out that evening with Maxwell Fordham. If he had then come back the next day and found Max in her room, they might have quarreled and Brian might have struck him.

"Brian told Jane that he had taken the train to Bristol on that Friday afternoon, had dinner near the station, and then gone to his hotel. I decided to check up on the timing. I went to Bristol and learned that Brian had checked into the hotel about eight o'clock that evening. So he *could* have been in Doughty Street at the time Max was killed. It doesn't take long to get to Bristol on the high-speed train. If he took a later train than he stated and didn't eat dinner until *after* checking into the hotel, he could have done it easily.

"At Bristol I learned that Brian had gone on to Bath, where I looked for him at his hotel. He was out, so I strolled around for a while and found him sitting in the square by the Abbey. We had met briefly long ago when Jane was in a seminar with me at the university, and he remembered me. When I asked him about his whereabouts on the day of the murder, he obviously resented my questioning but he man-aged to answer readily enough, insisting that he was on the train at four o'clock, as he had told Jane. I had no idea whether or not Brian was telling the truth, so I kept him on my list of suspects.

"Then I considered another possibility. When Jane and I

were having tea at the Savoy and saw that Lord Dodson observed Lady Muriel and Max together, it certainly gave Lord Dodson a motive for Max's murder, and subsequently it was possible that Lady Muriel might have quarreled with Max and struck him herself. Through your visit to them at Claridge's, we learned that both of them were in London and could have been in Jane's room at the time of the murder.

"Another factor in my suspicion of Lady Muriel had to do with that review which appeared in the *Apollo* magazine under Max's name, but which had been done by someone else, since Max was in Paris at the time of the concert. At Claridge's, Lady Muriel told you that she had come up to London several days before the fatal Friday, because there was a concert on Wednesday at the Royal Festival Hall which she particularly wanted to attend.

"This was the very concert about which the review was written. Now, it was possible that Lady Muriel shared her daughter's attitudes about contemporary music and had written the review herself. She was certainly knowledgeable about music, and if she had resumed an affair with Max, he might have asked her to do the review for him.

"This was merely a conjecture, of course, and it occurred to me that there was another possible candidate as the writer of the review. That was Sheila's friend, Fritz Morgan. Max had told Jane that Fritz had a sound musical training. They had even had an 'intelligent conversation' about Mozart one day. After all, Max had known nothing about Fritz and the drug smuggling until the day of his death. In the meantime, Sheila had been 'behaving like an angel.' How convenient it would have been for Max to nab the young man there in his own house and ask him to cover the concert for him. The brash and egocentric Fritz would have written whatever he liked about the music, with no consideration for Max's usual opinions.

"However, the language in the review made me wonder. Jane had told me that these were not only Patch's views but very nearly her own words. At first it seemed unlikely that Patch would have known Max well enough to be writing reviews for him. After all, she was only a schoolgirl when he knew her mother in the past, and Lady Muriel had obviously not seen him since that time until very recently.

"Then I began to wonder about an incident you had mentioned to me, Jane. You and Patch had gone to a performance of the Royal Ballet at the Opera House, where Max was present with his family. You noticed that when Patch saw the Fordham group, she showed considerable distress and turned rapidly away. You thought quite naturally that it was seeing Alan Fordham that had caused Patch to react painfully, assuming that her love affair of the previous summer had been with Jeremy, Alan's lover.

"It was certainly possible that Jeremy was going through a period of uncertainty about his sexual preferences, having an affair with a young woman and then turning to a relationship with Alan Fordham. However, Jane had met Max in September, and she noticed his hostility to his son not long after their acquaintance began. It seemed to me that the relationship between Alan and Jeremy had probably existed for some time. If an affair between Patch and Jeremy had ended in the summer, it would mean that Jeremy had conducted the affair during the time that he was also committed to Alan. From what Jane had described of the two young men, this seemed unlikely.

"Therefore, I wondered, could it have been seeing Max himself, not Alan, which had disturbed Patch on that occasion? If so, and if her affair had been with Max, it was much more likely that Patch herself might have done the review in the *Apollo* that echoed her opinions so strongly.

"Another factor also turned my attention to Patch. At the

hearing, James, your mother testified quite honestly that she could not positively identify the second voice in Jane's room on the day of the murder as that of either a man or a woman. It's true that if Max's voice was the one chiefly raised in anger, and the second person spoke softly, perhaps murmuring protests but not speaking loudly, it could be impossible to distinguish the sex of that person. But I remembered that Patch herself has a deep, almost gruff voice, the kind of voice that clearly belongs to a woman when you see her in person but which, on the telephone, for example, may be mistaken for that of a man. This ambiguity at least suggested to me that it might have been Patch with whom Max was quarreling that day.

"I was certain that if it had been Patch, she must have known nothing about Max's death. As we know now, she would never have allowed Jane to be falsely accused of the murder. It seemed to me there was one quite simple way to find out. I called her in Frankfort and asked her, feeling sure that if she was involved she would freely admit it, and of course that is what happened. When I first spoke to her, she was severely shocked. She told me at once that she had been in Jane's room that day but gave me no details, saying she would fly back to London immediately and go directly to Jane. I told her you were staying at the Edgar, Jane, and we know what happened from there."

"Poor Patch! It's been so dreadful for her."

Andrew refilled our drinks, and I said, "And now what about this thing with Fritz? How on earth did you manage that, and what does it mean for Patch?"

Andrew grinned. "It was just a lucky guess, really. And as for what it means legally, that's what we have to hear from James."

James smiled wryly. "That's not going to be as easy as you think. So tell us first how it came about."

Andrew took another swallow of his drink. "When I heard what Patch told you, Jane, about the events at the time of the murder, I noticed that she was surprised that the blow she struck could have been serious enough to cause a fatal blood clot. Now it is true that the pathologist said at the hearing that the blow need not be of great strength to have the rather unusual effect that resulted in Max's case, but common sense tells us that a seemingly light tap on the head would not very likely have fatal consequences. I asked a doctor, who confirmed that in his opinion the blow would have to have had significant force, although far less than that required for a fracture of the skull, for example.

"Then I wondered if someone else might have struck Max. The doctor also said that if a second blow was struck in the same spot as the first, it would not necessarily show up in the autopsy. At first, of course, I thought of Sheila Fordham. She admitted to being there at the time, and certainly she had a clear motive for preventing her father from turning Fritz in to the police. But then, I thought, the same motive applied equally to Fritz himself. Now I remembered the transcript we heard of Sheila's questioning by Inspector Kent when Fritz was arrested on the drug charge. When she begged her father not to report Fritz to the police, she said that he was standing there with some keys in his hand, saying, 'I must see Jane. I must return her keys.' And then he left. And what did Sheila say then? '*I rang up Fritz right away and told him what had happened.*'

"When I remembered this earlier today, I decided to ask Sheila about it. She was quite willing to talk to me. First I asked her if Fritz knew where Jane lived, and she said that he did because they had driven past Doughty Street and Wortle's Lane one day and she had told him that was where Daddy's girlfriend lived. Then she told me something that made me really take notice. She said that Fritz had told her he was sure

Jane wasn't guilty. She had paid little attention because Fritz was always sounding off about things, pretending to know more than he did. But I thought it would be worth trying an experiment, and as you saw tonight, we were lucky enough to bring it off.

I said, "Sheila certainly had me fooled tonight. That passionate kiss and all that sweet humility. I think she may have a real future in the theater!"

James and I congratulated Andrew on the success of his coup, and then I turned to James. "And now what happens to the charge against Patch?"

James's blue eyes clouded. "I only wish there were a simple answer to that. Offhand I would say that both Patch and Fritz are guilty of assault. I can certainly say that Fritz's belief that the one who struck first was to blame is inaccurate. He should have asked a solicitor, not a doctor. However, what will happen as to a charge of murder or manslaughter is anybody's guess. The police will inform Patch's solicitors of what has happened tonight, and they will work it out from there."

We talked on for a while and then the three of us walked back to my hotel, where I said good-bye to them both. In the morning I boarded my flight to California.

3 3

I had been at home in Los Angeles for nearly two weeks when I heard the final news about Patch. Fritz's admission to Sheila had given rise to a legal tangle of unusual complexity. Since there had been two blows to Max's head at the same point of contact, it was impossible to determine which had caused the fatal blood clot. Patch's counsel argued that since Fritz when he arrived saw no blood on Max's forehead but only the beginning of a swelling, the blood found on the body must have resulted from Fritz's blow.

In the end, both were charged with assault. Patch pleaded guilty and was given a suspended sentence. Fritz was convicted on two assault charges—one on Max and the other on Andrew. Inspector Kent reported that Fritz's fury at Andrew was chiefly because of Sheila's betrayal, not because of his admissions about Max. He still believed that he was clear of guilt in the attack on Max until he learned otherwise in court. He was also convicted on drug charges and was given a prison term on each count.

For Patch the relief was enormous. More than the fear of prison, she had been haunted by the belief that she had caused Max's death. Now she could believe that, whatever the legal technicalities, her blow to Max's head probably caused nothing more than a bruise. Fritz, with his compelling motive for murder and the fact that he was high on drugs, most probably dealt a heavy blow that was the real cause of Max's death.

I thought of the irony of Mrs. Hall's hearing Max's altercation with Patch but not his conversation with Fritz only moments later, but I knew that once she had closed the door and turned on the television she would have heard nothing more.

With the happy news of Patch's release I began to relax. I went to the beach to lie in the sun and swim, went to movies with old friends, and generally tried to keep occupied, but I was still unable to work on my project on Marius Hart.

"Give it time," said my father, "it will keep."

Each week I had a letter from James. For the most part his letters gave light and amusing accounts of his law cases. Brenda was doing excellent work and the clients were pleased with her. Was I beginning to recover from my ordeal? Wasn't it splendid news about Patch?

In my replies to James I could find little to say except to describe the sunny California weather, send greetings to him from my father, assure him that I was well, and add a hello to Brenda.

I had an occasional postcard from Andrew Quentin, who had gone on to Scotland. Then one day a letter arrived from the one person who had almost dropped out of my consciousness—Brian. He had finished his work in London and gone back to Connecticut. Now that he was going to be tenured, he and Linda were getting married.

"I'm glad you got out of that mess in London," the letter went on. "I bet your lawyer was glad you got off. I could tell he is really crazy about you, Janie. Hope things work out for you."

Poor Brian, I thought. Wrong to the last! And poor Linda—good luck to her. She would need it.

A few days later I heard from James again. When my father was in London he had invited James to come to visit us in Los Angeles whenever it might be convenient. Now James wrote that he would like to accept Dr. Winfield's kind invitation. Would the last week in May be agreeable? He had to remain in London until the twentieth for Brenda's wedding. She and her doctor had decided to make it legal, and James was to give away the bride.

My father and Gretchen were sitting on the patio when I read James's letter. In a glow I walked out to them, the letter in my hand, and told them what James had written. They beamed at each other and then at me.

"My dear girl," my father said to me, "that's the first real smile I've seen since you came home."

One evening two weeks later the three of us met James at the Los Angeles airport and brought him to the house, where we opened a bottle of champagne to welcome him. For an hour or more we enjoyed the pleasure of congenial conversation. Then Gretchen rose and suggested that my father drive her home. She said a cordial good-bye to James, and I went with her to my room to get her wrap.

The moment we were alone Gretchen turned to me with a smile. "James is absolutely delightful, Jane. You and Arthur have both told me that James was good and kind—but, my dear, you never said how attractive he is. He's really quite devastating!"

I looked at her joyfully. "Yes, he is, isn't he?"

I went out of the front door with Gretchen and waited until they drove away. Then I turned back through the entry and saw James staring out into the garden. He turned and looked at me and simply held out his arms. I flew to him and for a long moment he held me close to him. Then he kissed me with such passion and yet such tenderness that I felt my heart, like Shakespeare's lark, singing at heaven's gate.

Presently we wandered out into the garden, laughing at the absurdity of each not knowing that the other cared.

"When did you first—?" asked James.

I thought for a moment. "It was the day after I had had that letter from wretched Brian. I didn't know that I wanted you. My feet simply took me into Gray's Inn, and when you weren't there I felt utterly lost. Then you came along, and when you told me about the girl who had broken off with you, I remember thinking, How could she? Anyone lucky enough to have you—" I smiled at him. "And what about you?"

"Oh, I adored you from the first. When I took the receipt to you for the room rent and you opened the door, you looked at me with that sort of glowing smile and I thought, This girl is for me! But then you were friendly but so impersonal that I felt there was no hope. And of course, with Max in the picture—"

"Yes, of course. But James, ever since I met Brenda, I was sure you cared for her. She's so beautiful—"

"Brenda? Oh, she's a pretty little thing, isn't she? And clever, too. But not for me. But you know, darling, I did wonder about Andrew Quentin. He's a very good-looking chap, and you two have your shared interest in music. I know he lost his wife some time ago, and I thought, Perhaps he's ready to look about him—"

"Poor Andrew. No, he always seems perfectly cheerful and never bemoans his fate, but in fact I can see he's not ready to be interested in anyone yet. I hope someday he will be. He's so fine."

It was James's first visit to California, and for the week of his stay I took him on a round of all the tourist attractions, from Disneyland to Lake Arrowhead.

He reveled in the unremitting sunshine. "It's better than the south of France."

"But not with the same food." I giggled. "McDonald's Golden Arches will never compete with those little sidewalk cafés."

Now I found that all my interest in my project on Marius Hart came alive, and I was eager to get back to London and get on with it. James had a client who owned blocks of flats all over Bloomsbury, and he rang him up and arranged for me to rent one.

"I'll miss my piano at Doughty Street," I said with a smile.

James grinned. "Actually, darling, it's mine. I lived in your room when I was growing up. I was never much good at the piano but I rather enjoyed it. When I moved down to the basement flat, we left the piano where it was. So if you like, I'll have it sent round to your place when we get back."

I looked into those smiling blue eyes and laughed to myself, thinking, I don't believe in those old myths of a paradise on earth, but living in London with James in my life will surely come close.